Infantry Tank Warfare

(Revised and enlarged)

by

John Plant

D1521486

Published by New Generation Publishing in 2014

Copyright © John Plant 2014

First Edition

The author asserts the moral right under the Copyright, Designs
and Patents Act 1988 to be identified as the author of this work.

All Rights reserved. No part of this publication may be
reproduced, stored in a retrieval system or transmitted, in any
form or by any means without the prior consent of the author, nor
be otherwise circulated in any form of binding or cover other than
that which it is published and without a similar condition being
imposed on the subsequent purchaser.

www.newgeneration-publishing.com

 New Generation Publishing

Cover Photo: A Matilda II backs up to an early Cruiser

Dedicated to the memory of
the 13th/18th Royal Hussars

INFANTRY TANK WARFARE

Introduction

At the start of the Second World War all the major armies, with the arguable exception of the German army, were mistaken in their basic expectations for tanks. The result of this was that armoured units were badly organised and, in most cases, their vehicles were badly designed. During the course of the war these problems were largely overcome.

In the British army this mistaken process began around 1930 with the theoretical development of a form of armoured operations which may be termed 'Cruiser Tank Warfare'. This inevitably called forth a demand for a tank specifically designed for infantry support, the 'Infantry Tank'. At the time this seemed quite reasonably to be a continuation of the successful use of heavy tanks in the Great War and almost accidentally one of the Infantry Tanks became the best tank in France in 1940. However as the war ground on the idea became discredited and the employment of Infantry Tanks came to be much the same as that of Cruiser Tanks. The more difficult infantry support tasks were taken over by Specialised Armour, also in a separate but related process the infantry was given extra protection and mobility by the development of armoured personnel carriers. These processes will be studied in the following pages.

In general, over the years, the British Army has proceeded on commonsense lines and has not, as have some continental armies, been prone to fads created via the overheated imaginations of officers during peacetime. Its approach to tank warfare in the late 1930s was a case when this commonsense failed.

Chapter 1: Tactical Ideals

The operations of conventional warfare can take an infinite number of forms, it is this fact that makes the course of conventional operations difficult to predict. However for the sake of analysis it can be seen that there are two extreme cases of types of conventional operations. These are ideals and cannot exist in reality, in the real world the form operations take is on a sliding scale between the two extremes. One extreme can be termed 'Attrition Warfare', the other 'Mobile Warfare'. Neither of these expressions is really appropriate, but they will suffice for the purposes of this book.

In Attrition Warfare, operations can be expected to be infantry-based and their aim will be the destruction by battle of the enemy's forces. The forces may move a great deal but the purpose of that movement is purely to gain advantages for the next battle. Attrition Warfare operations, being infantry-based, can be expected to be slow in coming to a decision. It is one of their characteristics that, with the arms involved, like will fight against like, that is infantry will fight infantry, tanks against tanks, and the same with artillery.

In Mobile Warfare, operations will usually be AFV-based, their aim will be to manoeuvre against an enemy's critical point, when a 'critical point' is normally defined as a geographic location the loss of which will be disastrous for the enemy's fighting capacity. Capturing this critical point will throw the enemy's forces off balance, and once off balance they can be assaulted in such a way as to destroy their coherence.

It is possible, if unlikely, that the enemy is so badly deployed, and so weak, that there is no need to attack a critical point but dislocation attacks on his troops can start immediately. In either case attacks should be directed as much as possible against the enemy's logistic and command systems. This should result in mass surrenders, and enemy units that keep fighting will become immobile and either fall apart, or wait to be surrounded. This state was to be termed 'Strategic Paralysis'.

Speed is naturally a characteristic of Mobile Warfare. Another is that similar arms will not fight against each other. Tanks will not oppose tanks, but engage soft targets, and artillery will not pursue counter-battery duels.

Of course Mobile Warfare in its pure, ideal state cannot exist. Some fighting will always be necessary and fighting, even on a small scale, is a matter of attrition. The more the enemy fights, the less vulnerable is the critical point, and the more operations will bog down. Also critical points tend not to be that vulnerable. If the enemy is expecting his command structure to be attacked then his troops will be fully briefed as to what procedures to follow if the command structure fails. Similarly units will stockpile ammunition and other supplies in case the logistic system is destroyed. Such factors will tend to force Attrition Warfare on the attacker. However, even making every allowance for 'real world' considerations it can be seen that these are the two basic types of conventional operations.

It is but a small step from defining the two types of operations to defining the types of tanks best required to carry them out. Ideally there would be only one type capable of doing everything, but the resulting vehicle would be expensive and very probably only averagely good at what it did. Whereas vehicles designed specifically for one of the two types of operations may very well be cheaper and much better at their defined, and limited, role. Inevitably this kind of specialisation can be very tempting.

4

There was a further type of tank much seen before 1939, the light tank. This was not really a fighting vehicle and soon faded away. It will not be covered as a vehicle type, but will be occasionally mentioned in the text.

Basic thinking about the two different types of operations tanks may be involved in may be illustrated by a quote from the Field Service Regulations of 1935:

'Tanks are designed either to take part in mobile operations, for which speed and a wide circuit of action are essential at some sacrifice of armoured protection; or for close co-operation with infantry in the attack, for which armour is of more importance than speed or a wide circuit......Tanks of the former type are classified either as light or medium, are equipped with wireless for purposes of control and communication, and are organised into mixed and light tank battalions; those of the latter are called infantry tanks, and are organised into army tank battalions.'

The following study will consider the role of tanks in attrition warfare which, as attrition warfare is infantry based, was inevitably infantry support. The tanks were naturally described as 'Infantry Tanks'.

Chapter 2: The Great War

Early Days

Tanks were invented as a solution to requirements identified in 1915, being to flatten barbed wire entanglements and destroy MG posts. They were to assist the infantry to penetrate the German front line.

A committee was set up in February of that year to consider the problem. One remarkable thing about this committee was that it ignored the experience with armoured cars that the Royal Navy had gained in 1914 preferring instead to start from scratch. Initially it thought in terms of little more than a roller to flatten the wire, but with the impetus of war, made startling progress and in February 1916 the Mk I was produced. This was the basic design of the heavy tank and it altered only slightly before the end of the war, being produced in Marks I to V. There is no doubt that the production of the Mk I in such a short time was a great feat. The heavy tanks were the familiar large rhomboid-shaped tanks famous in WWI legend and the RTR cap badge. They were large, being roughly 26 feet long, eight high and 28 tons in weight, they were slow, mechanically unreliable and nearly blind, but could cross a nine foot trench. Initially they were called 'landships' or 'trench crossing machines,' then they were called 'water carriers' for security purposes, then 'tanks' as a shortened version of the same thing.

The tanks were designed and built in a creditably short time, but that inevitably resulted in teething troubles, and they were sent into action far too soon, however a greater criticism was that their deployment should have been delayed until there were enough to score a significant, if not decisive, victory. This concept may have sounded tempting but it would have required the High Command to stake an immense amount on a totally untried weapon when the manufacturing capacity of the country was already stretched to the limit. Conversely the Battle of the Somme was planned as the decisive battle of the war and Field Marshal Haig would have been obliged to throw every available resource into it.

Weapons alone, in this case tanks, do not make warfare but it is their use that does. British tank warfare can be said to have started when the drills were worked out and the plans drawn up for the deployment of 48 tanks on 15th September 1916 during the Battle of the Somme.

As tanks had been developed for a specific task, that of supporting the infantry forward in trench warfare, the principles of their use were obvious and the drills simple. They were to advance in line in front of the attacking infantry and arrive on the objective at the same time, however little went according to plan though the few tanks that made it to the German lines proved very effective.

British reports about the tanks were optimistic but the Germans were less impressed. Their infantry already had access to armour piercing (AP) ammunition that could defeat tank armour, and as the tanks moved so slowly they were vulnerable to artillery. Nevertheless, the fact that a British tank force existed in November 1917 was a tribute to the imagination and foresight of the British command. However as will be seen the events of that month were to change everything, but now an attempt must be made to describe the German defences that the tanks were built to defeat.

The battle of the Somme had been critical from the German point of view. This battle is usually remembered in England as a futile massacre of the attackers, but initially it also caused the Germans a large number of casualties. This was because the war had entered a new phase of attrition based on heavy artillery fire (*die Materialschlacht*), and German defensive tactics had to change to cope with it.

These changes started to occur almost of their own accord. The destructive effect of the *Materialschlacht* on trenches was so great that they were abandoned and the troops fought from shell holes, which were usually in front of the trench. The British procedure of improving shell holes and linking them to make trenches was resisted by the Germans. Doing that would have given the artillery a target. Counter-attacks, so much a feature of German defensive tactics, would still be put in as soon as possible after a position was lost.

However more systematic changes were needed, and these changes are commonly associated with Generals Hindenburg and Ludendorff who replaced General von Falkenhayn while the battle was raging. It is possible, though, that these changes were in hand before the change of command. The new German defensive measures consisted firstly, of the construction of a series of strong defensive lines ten to thirty miles behind the front line, and secondly they made revolutionary changes to their defensive tactics, changing them to a system of defence-in-depth.

Five defensive lines were planned, but priority was given to the construction of the 'Hindenburg Line' and this was undertaken by 15,000 labourers, mostly Germans, and 50,000 prisoners of war, mostly Russians. The other lines were traced but in general little work was done on them.

The new tactics were to be based on a series of zones: the forward one, the outpost zone, was 500 to 1,000 yards deep and would clarify the enemy's intentions, the battle zone would be up to 2,000 yards deep where the major fighting would take place, and the rearward zone would be as deep as was required for the artillery positions. Ideally the zones would be based on a series of ridges so that the attackers would pass over a ridge into the battle zone. They would then be out of the direct observation of their artillery but very much under the observation of the defender's. The defender's artillery would be pulled back as far as possible. Alternative battery positions would be dug and targets pre-registered. Troops would be positioned ready for counter-attacks. The principle of the defence was that the attackers would be stopped and shot to pieces by the artillery, then the infantry, who had remained safe in dug-outs or bunkers would put in a counter-attack that would bundle the surviving attackers back to their start line.

Trenches, though no longer basic to the defensive scheme, were to be retained. The living conditions in them were better than those in shell holes. Command was easier, and trenches facilitated movement, particularly that of the wounded. They gave the allied artillery something to shoot at, but were to be abandoned for battle.

The initial plan for the troops holding the line was that they should fall back in front of the attack then join in the counter-attack. This was asking a great deal of even the finest troops.

These tactics involving giving ground and counter-attacking were known as 'elastic defence' (*Das Elastische Kampfverfahren*) by the Germans. This type of defence could work well if the attackers were trying for a break-through, but if they were limiting their aims to a break-in, occupying the first crest, digging in and locating their artillery observers there, then inviting a counter-attack, then attrition might work in the attacker's favour.

However good elastic defence may have been in principle, in practice there was commonly too much reliance on strongpoints. These were based on villages or copses, farm buildings or other handy sites, and usually garrisoned by one or two companies of infantry. A defence based on a series of strongpoints with MG troops operating from shell holes between them, was much easier to set up than one based on zones, and would have looked attractive to local commanders.

The British found that strongpoints in the battle zone were often unexpectedly difficult to capture. This could be because British planning tended to concentrate on the assault of the German trenches, which left the troops tired and psychologically unprepared to tackle a new and unanticipated threat. Trenches were easy to see and photograph. Artillery could hit them with devastating accuracy, whereas strongpoints could be well enough fortified to be proof against field artillery. The assault of trenches could be rehearsed; strongholds required fieldcraft and leadership. Leadership was much harder if the attacking units had become mixed up, as so often happened. All this could disrupt the standard British advance by phase lines.

The situation could be complicated by the construction of pillboxes. Such concrete fortifications would be proof against artillery so a creeping barrage would pass over them leaving them still a threat and the attacking troops following the barrage would have to storm them, but that would result in them losing the barrage. These factors all affected, to one degree or another, the defence that the tanks were to be called on to defeat.

Not surprisingly the tanks were most effective when doing the job they had been designed for, which was attacking trenches, flattening barbed wire, engaging MGs and generally escorting the infantry forward. When confronted by the German defensive zones they were not so useful, striking out, as it were, into thin air, but they did attract fire away from the infantry and they were useful against pillboxes. As the German defences became more ad-hoc and dependent on strongpoints, so tanks, having something to aim at, became more useful. In view of this it is not surprising that views of the effectiveness of tanks should vary so widely, particularly as, it seems, British commanders did not always fully appreciate the nature of German defensive tactics.

In many ways the strengths and weaknesses of tanks in the Great War were demonstrated in the Battle of Cambrai.

The Battle of Cambrai

The Passchendaele offensive was the major British military effort of 1917. As it ground to a halt two officers independently recommended an offensive further to the south, at Cambrai. These officers were General Tudor, commanding the artillery of a division near Cambrai, and General Elles, commanding the Tank Corps. They were not the first to notice the potentialities of this area, and earlier preliminary studies had been carried out but these had not led to action.

In this sector the Hindenburg Line, as in most other sectors, was laid out and largely constructed before elastic defence was fully understood and it had to be modified in something of a rush before it could be occupied. It consisted essentially of what the Official History calls the Support System. This was reinforced by digging the Hindenburg Front Trench System, running through Banteux, around 1000 yards in front of it on a reverse slope. The space between these two trench lines was the Battle Zone. Again, around 500 yards in front of the Front Trench System was dug the Outpost Line, running through La Vacquerie, again on a reverse slope. This was the outer limit of the Outpost Zone. Because of the lack of time these systems had not been completed, and the large number of bunkers and battery positions required for elastic defence had not been built. Some villages and farms in the outpost and battle zones were prepared for defence, and also some in the rearward zone, but, remarkably, not Fontaine or Bourlon. *(See Sketch 1)*

The essence of the plans put forwards by both generals was that an attack could be made by surprise. Up to that point the long preliminary bombardment had precluded surprise, and such a bombardment was necessary to destroy the barbed wire. Technology had improved this situation. A new fuze had been issued which caused the shells to explode instantly upon hitting anything rather than burying themselves in the ground before exploding. This made the artillery much more effective particularly against barbed wire. Also up to this time guns had to be registered on their targets. This naturally forfeited surprise, but now techniques had been developed to make registration unnecessary so the start of the barrage could not be anticipated. Further the use of tanks would also facilitate surprise, and they could take on much of the barbed wire flattening task.

The battle plan involved attacking roughly between two canals, the Canal du Nord, largely dry, and the St Quentin Canal. Initially the idea was purely a raid to penetrate the Hindenburg Line with tanks, let the cavalry through for a *grande chevauchee*, cause plenty of casualties and damage for little cost, and pull back to the start line. Unfortunately, as was often the trend in the Great War, its aims became more ambitious. The first paragraph of the 3rd Army orders was:

"The object of the operation is to break the enemy's defensive system by a coup de main; with the assistance of tanks to pass the Cavalry Corps through the break thus made: to seize Cambrai, Bourlon Wood, and the passages over the Sensee River and to cut off the troops holding the German front line between Havrincourt and that river."

There can be little doubt that the objectives for exploitation after the front line had been broken were not well thought out, but no doubt achieving them would force the Germans to abandon a substantial section of the Hindenburg Line. Field Marshal Haig made it plain that if significant progress was not being made within 48 hours the offensive should be closed down. Because of the necessity of sending troops to Italy he was not in a position to be drawn into a long-running battle also, and probably more importantly, after 48 hours German reinforcements would start to arrive from other sectors of the line. The initial tactical requirement in his view was the capture of Bourlon village and wood, the high ground that dominated the battlefield, and he suggested the creation of a special all-arms force to do that. This suggestion, and it is remarkable that it was no more than that, was ignored by 3rd Army. The importance of this high ground does not seem to have been realised, instead of being rushed by a dedicated unit, it was to be captured by the troops breaking the line. The cavalry was to cross the St Quentin Canal between Marcoing and Masnieres, cross the Masnieres-Beaurevoir Line, then ride off to Cambrai. Although 3rd Army expected the cavalry to capture Cambrai, Haig only expected it to surround it. Perhaps, following its disastrous experience at Monchy le Preux seven months earlier, the cavalry would have preferred the Haig option. After that an advance on the Sensee would start.

The Battle can be seen as falling into two parts; the British attack and the German counter-attack. Only the first part will be considered in this chapter, and this, the British attack, breaks down into three tactical phases. The first, accomplished in the first few hours, was the passage of the Hindenburg Line. The second was the capture of Bourlon village and wood, and the St Quentin canal crossings. The third was the exploitation by cavalry east to Cambrai and north to the Sensee.

The assault on the Hindenburg Line trenches went remarkably smoothly. It took place on 20th November 1917. The barrage, provided by 1003 guns and howitzers, started at 6.20 am, and shortly afterwards around 200 tanks attacked. The German trenches were wider than usual, specifically designed to make anti-tank obstacles, but this problem was overcome by the tanks carrying large fascines of brushwood that were dropped into the trenches for the tanks to drive over.

Surprise was so complete that the Germans did not manage any significant immediate counter-attacks, but some batteries in the battle zone that had been missed by the British barrage were able to inflict some casualties on the tanks as they came over the front trench system. In fact the Germans hardly fought for the trenches, but they did fight for some small strongpoints in the battle zone, usually defended farms. There was determined resistance at two points only. One was Havrincourt, but the most important was Flesquieres.

Here occurred the massacre of around a dozen tanks. Flesquieres was on a slight ridge and some concrete MG posts had been built into its ruins. The attacking tanks and infantry halted, for around 40 minutes to reorganise, at a physically insignificant feature called 'Le Grand Ravin', and this halt gave the defenders time to prepare. An understrength field battery was deployed in the open behind the ridge. As the advance resumed the MGs kept the infantry back, and the tanks, instead of attacking in line abreast through the wire, drove in line astern up a sunken road onto the open ridge. The battery destroyed them, one after the other as they came into view. *(see note)* Flesquieres was still in German hands at sunset. The attacking infantry division, the 51st Highland Division, did not recover its momentum for the rest of the day, probably because its HQ was over seven miles away from Flesquieres.

14

This disaster might have been small change in terms of the assault as a whole, but it retarded the advance on Bourlon Wood and, with darkness falling at 4.03, that was enough to prevent this objective being reached.

The end of the first day seemed to show a great success, but it was a meretricious one. It is true that phase one had been a great success, but not phase two. Bourlon wood had not been reached and the canal crossings had not been seized. The great characteristic of cavalry is its mobility, but here it was defeated by a steep-sided and deep canal covered by MGs. Actually there was a small bridge that horsemen could have crossed on but, due to the friction of war, it was missed. Phase two had failed.

Phase three was dependent on the cavalry crossing the canal so could not really start. There was one cavalry division which advanced by a different route but because of its timetable being set back by the Flesquieres disaster, and because of an apparent excess of caution, it made no real progress.

At the end of the day around 175 tanks were out of action, though only a minority due to enemy action. It was fortunate that the Germans had no troops available for a deliberate counter-attack. They were, though, already on their way.

The second day showed the startling lack of contingency planning. The cavalry had failed to cross the canal and it was a bit vague what else it was expected to do. Likewise there was a lack of drive in the move against Bourlon Wood, but there was a success in the form of the capture of Fontaine. The next day a German counter-attack recaptured Fontaine. The British approach to Fontaine seems a little lackadaisical. It was believed that if Bourlon were taken, Fontaine would fall of its own accord. This proposition was never proven. As German reinforcements arrived they were fed into the front around Bourlon Wood and along the Masnieres-Beaurevoir Line.

The 23rd November saw bitter, but inconclusive, fighting in Bourlon Wood. Only 16 tanks could be assembled for it, and they were not a success in such a close environment. There was a tank-led assault on Fontaine, and here also the tanks fared badly, the German infantry quickly realising the tank's weak points. The first part of the battle was halted in time for the second to start on 30th November.

The lessons of the battle were there for all to see. The obvious one was that with the tank, improved artillery techniques and firm going, the German front line could fairly easily be pierced. This lesson had been learned before, but it was greatly magnified at Cambrai. Unfortunately the difficulties of converting a break-in to a break-out were as intractable as ever. The main difficulties can be listed as:

a) Infantry tire quickly. The psychological stress and pure hard work of infantry fighting means that not too much can be demanded of them. It was too much to ask of the troops breaking the line to go as far as Bourlon Wood. This might have been a job for a cavalry division, and if this had been tried it would have almost certainly have succeeded.

b) The limitation of tanks. They were not wonder weapons. The strength of tank units fell away quickly. They were of limited use in woods and built up areas. Two thirds of the available tanks were used on the first day. It may have been better if this fraction had been smaller to allow greater offensive power on subsequent days. One tank trying to cross the St Quentin canal collapsed the bridge thus making the cavalry advance much more difficult.

c) The cavalry failed. Cavalry was the only instrument

available for the exploitation of a tactical success, but its day had passed. After 20th November a reaction against cavalry set in and a program was started to convert cavalry regiments to cyclists or less mobile roles. This was a pity because cavalry could be very useful on the defensive, and performed well during the German Spring Offensive of 1918. In fact some units were hurriedly re-horsed for this. The future, though, inevitably lay with petrol.

d) Communications always broke down. In the Great War communications depended upon telephone lines. These were even harder to maintain at Cambrai than at other battles because they were so often cut by the tanks. Even lines high above roads could be snagged by fascines. The problem was to a degree obviated in the Second World War by the widespread issue of radios.

e) Despite the assault achieving total surprise the Germans reacted quickly even though some of their units were poor quality (*Landwehr*). This was partly because of the nature of elastic defence which involved a high degree of contingency planning, and partly because of the wide variety of field fortifications available, for instance the Masnieres-Beaurevoir Line.

Remarkably the difficulties of Phase two, converting a break-in to a break-out, were anticipated by Sir William Tritton, the managing director of William Foster & Co the tank builders, when he observed the tank assault of Thiepval on 22nd September 1916, only a week after the first ever deployment of tanks in war. He immediately initiated the process for the design and manufacture of what were to be classified as medium tanks.

The mediums, which were significantly faster then the heavy tanks, were first used on 26th March 1918 and they showed themselves to be very useful on the battlefield. Unfortunately attempts to use them in cooperation with cavalry were not a success and the war ended before they could be used to force a break-out.

Note:
This action was to become famous. Field-Marshal Haig wrote in his dispatch: '*Many of the hits upon our tanks at Flesquieres were obtained by a German artillery officer who, remaining alone at his battery, served a field gun single-handed until killed at his gun. The great bravery of this officer aroused the admiration of all ranks.*' Long after the war the Germans raised a statue to the officer said to be involved.

However modern authors no longer take this story seriously observing that the guns were withdrawn when they ran out of ammunition.

German Anti-Tank Tactics

After Cambrai the Germans naturally started to take AT defence much more seriously. The battle itself had shown some major aspects of AT defence which were pointers to the future.

The action at Flesquieres had shown how tanks were vulnerable to artillery in the direct fire mode, what would later be termed an 'AT screen', or *'PAK front'*, but should also have shown how vulnerable the AT screen was to artillery fire or air attack.

The fact that tanks could make no progress in Bourlon Wood or Fontaine showed how vulnerable they were in close country. The German infantry, having driven off the British infantry, attacked the tanks at close range with AP ammunition and bundles of grenades. In Fontaine they attacked the roofs of the tanks from upstairs windows. In Bourlon Wood a design fault of the tanks proved disastrous. Many of the trees had been reduced to stumps, when a tank drove over one its belly plate bent upwards and snagged the fly wheel. This stalled the engine, which in the tactical conditions it was not possible to restart.

On the third day of the battle a new AT measure made itself felt, *K flak (Kraftfahr-Fliegerabwehrkanone)*. These were AA guns, usually 57-mm, mounted on lorries, and they could be devastating against tanks. They had a very limited off-road mobility, but because of the poor communications of the day they were almost impossible to engage with artillery, and because the tanks were almost blind, they could not defend themselves against them. *K flak* claimed a total of 64 tanks. In future years this type of vehicle would be called a 'tank destroyer' and would be one of the principal AT weapons. At the time the British, at least, attached no particular significance to them.

The Germans quickly set to work to produce new AT weapons. The two main ones were an AT rifle and an AT gun. The rifle was really just a scaled up service rifle. It was of 13-mm calibre, big and heavy, unpopular and not very effective. The gun was small, 37-mm, cheap and handy. Its muzzle velocity was not that high but quite good enough for the thin armour of the tanks of the time. The plan was to deploy these guns in AT forts scattered in the battle zone.

The Germans made a start on developing AT mines, but did not get very far. They did, however improve on their field AT fortifications. Even before Cambrai, as has been seen, they had widened certain trenches to make them obstacles for tanks, but they also dug short trenches at right angles to the front and camouflaged them to make tank traps, pitfalls that the mammoth-like tanks would fall into. There were cases of streams being dammed to make inundations, and also the casting of concrete obstacles.

The Germans assumed that any significant Allied offensive would be led by tanks and they gave the fight against them priority, but this had an important indirect effect on the German defences. In order to have guns available for the direct fire role a large number was moved forward and dug

19

in around the forward edge of the battle zone. Such guns were no longer available for normal artillery employment, and they suffered heavy casualties.

It could well be that the Germans had the measure of the tanks of 1918 and, if their army had not been worn away in the great Spring Offensive, they could have defeated a major tank-led offensive providing they had time to select the battlefield and prepare their defences. But after the failure of the Spring Offensive they fell back through a series of positions based on rivers, these being good AT obstacles. However rivers run in valleys which could be dominated by British artillery, and these positions crumbled one after the other.

Chapter 3: The Inter-War Years

The end of the Great War saw the end of the development of the heavy tanks and, as these tanks were scrapped so the tactics that had been developed for then became obsolete. With the end of the 'war to end war' it is not surprising that the study of tank tactics was allowed to lapse and little interest was shown in tanks by the infantry until 1923 when the 'Vickers' Medium Tank was issued in significant numbers.

The major problem was how the tanks could best help the infantry forward in view of the now significant difference between the speed and mobility of the tank and the infantryman. Two main types of deployment were considered: in one the tanks would attack the enemy's flanks and rear, working in cooperation with the infantry but not actually accompanying them, while in the other they would directly support the infantry. However, in order to avoid moving slowly and offering the defending artillery easy targets they would start their advance well behind the infantry, timed to arrive on the objective at the same time.

These two deployments, in a tank-heavy assault, were summarised in the Field Service Regulations[1] of 1935:
'Tanks attacking as the main assaulting arm in direct co-operation with infantry may use the same lines of advance as the infantry or may attack from a flank (i.e. at right angles or obliquely to the lines of advance of the infantry) according to the existence of wire, to the suitability of the ground for movement and supporting fire, and the opportunities for surprise. In order to ensure co-operation between the artillery, infantry and tanks taking part in the attack, the following must be settled: the starting line of the infantry, the starting line of the tanks, the time at which each will cross their starting lines and the

pace at which each will move to their objective. Tanks should seldom be required to halt on a starting line. They should be brought, if possible, direct into the attack from an assembly position under cover, crossing a starting or check line at a given hour, but without a halt. The closer the infantry can follow the tanks on to the objective, the better; it can then take full advantage of the confusion created by the tank attack, and can take over the ground gained by the tanks without delay. It may sometimes be advisable for the infantry advance to start before the tank attack is actually launched, so that the infantry can work forward to suitable positions within striking distance of the objective. Such action may also serve to cover the advance of the tanks. If this method is adopted, sufficient covering fire for the infantry must be provided to make its advance feasible.'

There was the question of what were the tanks to do once the enemy's front line had been secured. The medium tanks of the time were thinly armoured and had to keep moving to survive, so perhaps imaginative use could have been made of them. The following is an account of an exercise printed in a German manual of 1927[2]. It may be commented that it is a pity that an English translation was not published.

'If the hostile position, or line, to be assaulted is a significant distance away then the infantry must work its way forward to reduce the storming distance to the minimum possible. This will have the effect of reducing, as much as possible, any danger they might be in if they have to fall back to their start line.

The tanks' start line, because of their greater speed and armour protection against artillery, will be far to the rear of that for the infantry. Consequently while the infantry is working its way forward the tanks, drawn up in their assaulting formation, starting from the rear and travelling faster, will overtake the infantry and break into the enemy's defensive zone. In order to arrive together on the edge of

22

the zone this assaulting distance should not be more than a few hundred meters, and the greatest possible speed developed to enable the infantry to secure the objective. In continuing the assault, possibly some of the tanks, having broken through the enemy's defences, will immediately continue their advance to make a deep penetration, leaving their infantry behind. The remainder of the tanks will assist the infantry in mopping up the enemy's remaining MG and infantry positions.

Because of the depth of the defensive zone, and the random siting of the defensive positions, which will result in the tanks advancing in sideways and diagonal directions, it is probably that the tanks will advance at top speed by bounds. However forward progress will be slow and the infantry, supported by tanks, will have to widen the gap.

This seems to be the way that the frontal attack is viewed by the English.'

Neither of these deployments outlined above seemed totally satisfactory to the infantry who came to prefer the concept of small AFVs dedicated to their support.

An attempt was made to meet this requirement with light tanks, which started to be issued in 1929. They were to be used as mobile MG posts. This was not judged a success, largely because of the poor obstacle crossing ability, but the idea was a good one and would spawn the Universal Carrier, usually known as the 'Bren Gun Carrier', and was found to be very useful throughout the Second World War, but not in the light tank role.

Throughout the 1920s in the British army progress on infantry support and the AFVs required had been slow, but in 1931 the important manual, 'Modern Formations', was published. The purpose of this manual was to define the campaign-winning manoeuvres of masses of what would be termed 'Cruiser Tanks'. These masses would not be used for infantry support which would require specialised, and not very sophisticated, vehicles. The manual almost looked down on them: *'Armour will naturally have its place since it can be carried in any mechanical vehicle, but the machines to be provided for infantry will be different from those assigned to the tank arm. Infantry machines need not be fast, and they must be small so as to be capable of easy concealment. In the enclosed types of country in which alone infantry will normally operate offensively, concealment of such machines will be available.'*

Not surprisingly with the RTC now committed the wide ranging manoeuvre warfare, it was not until 1936 that a dedicated infantry support tank was issued.

Infantry support, by its very nature, requires tanks of different characteristics than those of Cruiser Tanks. An Infantry tank ('I' tank) must be thickly armoured, but need not run much faster than a man on foot. Its armament was to be debated, but settled down to being the same as for Cruisers. The vehicles themselves will be considered in the next chapter. They were to be organised in Army tank battalions separately from Cruiser Tanks. Even though the first Infantry Tanks were not issued until1936, what was expected of these battalions was laid down in the same Field Service Regulations already quoted, those of 1935:

'Army tank battalions are equipped with heavily armoured tanks, which are somewhat slower than medium tanks; they are also provided with a small number of light tanks for purposes of control and intercommunication within the battalion. Army tank battalions are intended for close co-operation with infantry in the attack and counter-attack. They are required to break down wire entanglements and to destroy or neutralize machine guns. They are a valuable aid to gaining the advantages of surprise and initial success in the attack and to maintaining its momentum. They also

provide a most efficient means of countering hostile tanks. Their success will depend on the choice of suitable ground, on the concealment of their assembly and approach, and on the co-operation of other arms in giving early warning of the existence of tank obstacles and in neutralizing the fire of hostile anti-tank weapons.'

Until the tanks were issued and procedures worked out for their use, this paragraph must have been regarded as visionary, however it does show that the Infantry Tank concept was in no way revolutionary, but rather harked back to 1918.

Notes:
1) Field Service Regulations, Vol II, Operations – General. Quotes from Chapters IV and I
2) Taschenbuch der Tanks, Erganzungsband 1927, Fritz Heigl.

Chapter 4: The Tanks

Because of the specialised and limited nature of infantry support it is not surprising that there were fewer different models of infantry tank produced than there were of Cruiser tanks. It should be noted that tanks supplied by the USA could not be described as infantry tanks. There were only four marks of British infantry tanks, though as will be seen when specialised armour is considered, each mark could spawn many variants.

The great step forward towards the start of infantry tank production was made when General Sir Hugh Elles was appointed to the post of Master General of the Ordnance. He had commanded the Royal Tank Corps on the western front in the Great War and believed that the correct and most effective use of tanks was in infantry support, as they had been used at Cambrai. In 1934 he asked Major-General Hobart, who was the Inspector of the Tank Corps to come up with a draft specification for an infantry support tank. It may be doubted if General Hobart, who was a dedicated tankman and was capable of showing contempt for the other arms, was the right man for this task. The result was two specifications which turned out to be descriptions of what would be the Infantry Tanks Mk I and Mk II, commonly known as Matildas I and II. Development on Matilda I started almost immediately.

The A11 Infantry Tank Mk I (Matilda I) was first supplied in 1936. Its most notable feature was its cheapness, but it was not a generally useful vehicle. In 1939 it was obsolescent. Only 139 were built. It was small, 16 feet long and just over six foot high. It had a crew of two and its only armament was one MG. The basic idea for this tank seems to have been General Hobart's concept of a large number of small tanks being able to swamp a defence.

The RTC was not pleased with the Matilda I. The corps wanted each tank to mount a real gun, and in 1937 the A12 Infantry Tank Mk II (Matilda II) was ordered. The specification was a variation of the Medium Tank A7 specification, with thicker armour. It was ordered 'off the drawing board', which indicated a degree of panic to get a tank into production but was a procedure which, because of lack of troop trials, would cause a lot of trouble with other tanks. However it worked well with Matilda II. As with Cruiser Tanks, 'I' Tanks usually had a Close Support (CS) version. The Matilda II CS had a three inch howitzer.

The tank looked a winner. It was not large, being 18 feet 5 inches long and eight feet high, but its thick cast armour gave it a monolithic appearance. It had a three-man turret and mounted a 2-pdr as did contemporary Cruisers. Its thick armour gave it a reputation of being 'invulnerable on the battlefield' and it was the best tank in France in 1940 even if it was a little too heavy for the steering, which resulted in frequent clutch failures. It dominated the early desert fighting until the Germans stopped it with large calibre AT guns in the Battleaxe offensive of 1941.

The Matilda II suffered, as did all British tanks of the time, in that, having a narrow turret ring, it could not be up-gunned, and soon the 2-pdr was obsolete. Production ceased in 1943, by which time nearly 3,000 had been made. Remarkably some were sent to the USSR. It is not known what the Russians thought of it.

The Infantry Tank Mk III ('Valentine'-see note) was developed as a private venture by Vickers. Hence no 'A' number. It bears a resemblance to the A9 Cruisers, but had much thicker armour, up to 65-mms thick. Its top speed, 15mph, was only half that of the Cruiser.

When first produced it was turned down by the War Office,

but as the requirement to supplement the Matilda II production became urgent, this decision was reversed.

Its first engine, a petrol engine, was found to be unreliable. After it had been replaced by a diesel engine the tank gained a good reputation for reliability. It was up-gunned from 2-pdr to 6-pdr, then 75-mm. The early turrets had crews of two, the commander having to double as loader. Later versions had three man turrets which, with the bigger guns, must have been difficult to operate. There was no CS version.

The Valentine went out of production in 1944, 8,275 having been made, more than any other British tank.

The A22 (initially A20) Infantry tank Mk IV, the Churchill was the most successful British tank of the war. Its original specification called for something which would not have seemed out of place in 1918. The Mk I version had a 2-pdr in its turret and a 3-in howitzer in its hull. There was a CS version with the position of these two guns reversed. The choice of armament may seem odd. It was based on the same thinking as for the French Char B, a high velocity gun in the turret for destroying concrete obstacles, and a large calibre gun in the hull firing HE to blast away earthworks. When the original specification was drawn up the British army was almost in awe of the French, but this was to change. In some early models the hull howitzer was replaced by another 2-pdr, but finally by an MG. As the Churchill was expected to function like a Great War heavy tank there were initially an MG on either side of the hull, under the top run of the tracks. These were to fire sideways along the trenches as the tanks crossed them. This was another idea that was abandoned.

The Churchill was first issued in 1941 but unfortunately it had been rushed into production and suffered from extensive mechanical faults which took years to correct. Its original main armament was obviously insufficient and a 6-pdr was mounted in the turret, the specification was altered to do away with the hull mounted gun.

As the war ground on the 6-pdr was often replaced by a 75-mm, sometimes carried out as a local modification using the 75-mm guns taken off Sherman wrecks. Also there was a CS version with a 95-mm gun. Remarkably, during the NW Europe campaign, when APDS ammunition became available for the 6-pdr some Churchill's, ideally one per troop, had their 6-pdrs re-mounted to provide an improved AT capacity. The Infantry tank, it can be seen, finished up with much the same armament as the Cruiser.

The Churchill armour was thick, up to 102-mm in most marks, but up to 152-mm in later ones. This was actually thicker than the glacis of the Tiger II, but it was vertical whereas the German designers had noticed the advantage of sloped armour. Its thick armour made the Churchill almost impervious to the panzerfaust.

The Churchill was a highly effective Infantry Tank, but probably its greatest contribution was as a basic hull for specialised armour designs, which will be covered in a later chapter. The success of the Churchill is shown by the fact that 5,640 were built.

One particularly welcome aspect of the Churchill was that it was surprisingly mobile. It could cross obstacles that would stop other tanks. It is worth a few lines to consider the properties that aid a tank's mobility.

The obvious one is the length of track on the ground. For best obstacle crossing the tank should be long and thin. Unfortunately if the tank were too long as compared to its width it would be impossible to steer. In general it has been found that the length of track on the ground should not exceed 1.8 times the distance apart of the centre of the track.

This worked out well for Churchills which were not expected to be agile.

Wherever possible the centre of gravity of the tank should be as low as possible, and the light tanks and the Vickers Mediums failed in this respect.

The track links should have deep grips. In this respect the Matilda II failed. Its track links were flat with 'H' shaped indentations, whereas those on the Churchill were excellent, but it did mean that they destroyed any road they drove along.

The tracks should be supported along the entire length they were in contact with the ground. This was largely achieved by the Churchill with its large number of small road wheels. The Germans tried to achieve the same in the Panther and Tiger with overlapping road wheels. By contrast, a small number of large road wheels, as seen on the early Cruisers, is more efficient for running on roads.

It was these considerations that gave the Churchill its excellent mobility.

Some Vital Statistics (CS versions ignored)

		Date	Weight Tons	Crew	Armament			Armour Mm (max)	Speed mph
					Main	MGs coax	hull		
A11	Matilda I	1936	11	2		1	-	60	8
A12	Matilda II	1939	26	4	2-pdr	1	-	78	15
Valentine	MkI,III	1939	16	3or4	2-pdr	1	-	65	15
	Mk IX	1942		4	6-pdr	0 or 1	-		
	Mk X	1943		4	75-m	1			
A22 Churchill	MkI	1941	38.5	5	2-pdr	1	3-in How	102	15
	MkIII	1942			6-pdr	1	1		
	MkVII	1944	40		75-m	1	1	152	

These were the four 'I' tanks that saw action. Others were developed to one degree or another, but were judged to be failures and have been ignored here.

Also extensively used for infantry support:

Sherman	1942	31	5	75-mm 1	1	76	29
Firefly	1944	32	4	17-pdr 1	-	76	29

In 1944 Field Marshal Montgomery requested the development of a 'Capital Tank' to replace the Cruiser and Infantry types. The result was the Centurion. It was originally classified as a Heavy Cruiser but soon came to be termed a 'Main Battle Tank'.

Centurion I	1945	47	4	17-pdr 1	-	127	32

with an alternative coax of a 20-mm cannon

Note

There is some controversy over the origin of the name 'Valentine,' there are three theories:

a) It was one of the Christian names of the designer, Sir John V Carden. He had been killed in an air crash and the tank was named in his honour.

31

b) The prototype was accepted on 14th February 1940, St Valentine's Day.

c) It was an acronym of 'Vickers Armstrong Limited, Elswick, Newcastle-upon-Tyne.'

While this controversy is of no importance it does illustrate how even the simplest aspects of Tank Warfare can be difficult to pin down.

Tactics

The Infantry Tank tactics of 1935 have been described in Chapter 3, they were to change significantly by 1939. There were two causes for this change. The first was the nature of the tank, particularly its thick armour which was expected to make it very difficult to stop. The second was an appreciation of the great depth of German defences, which was usually taken to be 1,000 yards.

The change involved some tanks driving ahead of the infantry so to be able to be engaging the enemy's defences throughout their entire depth at the same time as the infantry, supported by other tanks, was fighting in the enemy's front line. The aim was for the total disruption of the enemy's defence.

There are two significant points about this tactic. The first was that, because of the expansion of the army and the issue of new equipment, the army did not manage to hold large scale exercises to test it. Secondly was that this tactic could only work while AT weapons were inadequate, and, under the incentive of war, that would quickly change.

The Infantry Tank tactics of 1939 are best illustrated by a series of quotes from the 1939 manual 'Tactical Handling of Army Tank Battalions'[1].

'Section 1. – The Army Tank Battalion

1. Function

Army Tank Battalions are army troops organized, equipped and trained for employment with formations of all arms.

Army tank units are equipped with tanks possessing heavy armour, relatively low speed and high obstacle-crossing power. They have no weapons for their own close support other than smoke projectors, nor have they special reconnaissance sections. Thus they are not designed to act independently but in co-operation with infantry and artillery

By virtue of its high degree of fire power, mobility and protection, the infantry tank is pre-eminently an offensive weapon of great effect in battle.'

'In the execution of his attack he can best defeat the defence by pushing in with the greatest rapidity compatible with the effective co-operation of all arms. The components of the attack should fall upon the defence in rapid succession; the artillery covering fire should be closely followed by tanks which, in their turn, should be closely followed by the infantry.'

'Section 5. Attack

1. General. – Army tanks are essentially an arm of attack to be used to precede and accompany infantry in the attack against wired and prepared defences. Whatever the tactical role of the force to which they are allotted, the tanks' part should be offensive action to assist the infantry. Full advantage will not be gained from their characteristics and their special qualities in attack if employed in a static role and they should not be so used except in very exceptional circumstances.'

'8. The tank advance. – The attacking tanks must be deployed as near the infantry start line as possible.

Suitable formations for advance are considered below. The formation must be dense enough to enable the tanks to search the ground thoroughly yet open enough to allow of sufficient room for minor manoeuvre against anti-tank guns. There must be sufficient depth to ensure that enemy machine guns, missed through casualties or change of direction of leading tanks, are dealt with by following tanks: there must also be local reserves to tanks.

As the defence will generally be protected by wire entanglements, the density of tanks is also influenced by the necessity of making sufficient breaches in the wire for the infantry.

In an advance against organized defences, the first echelon precedes the infantry. Its task is:-
  (1) To fall upon the enemy on the frontage of attack before he has time to recover from the fire of supporting weapons.
  (2) To neutralize the automatic weapons in its zone of action in order to allow the infantry to advance.

In consequence, this echelon must have sufficient depth to enable these tasks to be carried out and to allow of mutual support between sections both laterally and in depth.

The leading sections must close with the enemy before he has time to recover from the action of the artillery. The rearmost sections must regulate their pace to that of the infantry and endeavour to neutralize all enemy small arms fire left by the leading sections.

The second echelon should move normally in rear of the advancing infantry. They must be prepared to move at once in front or to the flank of the infantry in order to deal with any short range small arms fire causing checks to the latter.

Against unorganised resistance and in certain types of

34

ground favourable to an infantry advance but unfavourable to tanks, the first echelon of tanks may follow the leading infantry. In this case their role will be similar to that of the second echelon tanks employed against organized resistance.

The battalion commander will retain a local reserve for use against the unexpected, maintenance of momentum and the local exploitation of success.

Woods and villages present special difficulties. Tanks are unable to neutralize enemy who take refuge in buildings or in thick cover and are themselves vulnerable to anti-tank weapons at short range. They therefore operate under severe disadvantages. Such localities are, however, easily identified on the ground and on the map and, if not too large, provide targets which can be dealt with comparatively easily by artillery fire and this should be the normal means of neutralizing the fire of their defenders.

Experience proved that a defender often clings stoutly to localities of this kind, however intense the artillery covering fire, and the attacking infantry will be held up until assistance of close support weapons or tanks is forthcoming.

Tanks should not pass enclosed localities until they are certain that fire from them is not holding up the infantry advance. If strongly held it may be necessary for tanks to deal with them to enable the infantry to effect a footing. The first essential is to neutralize the enemy fire coming from the edge of the enclosure.

9. The infantry advance. – In selecting the infantry start line and the formation in which leading infantry are formed up before the start it must be remembered that hostile defensive fire is certain to come down as soon as the enemy hears or sees the tanks or when supporting artillery fire begins.

The infantry should as a rule advance as close behind the leading tanks as it is possible for them to do. The closer they can keep the safer for both arms as they will be able to tackle the machine gun which has gone to ground to avoid the tanks before it has been able to come to life again, and to assist the tanks by bringing fire to bear on hostile anti-tank guns which have not been effectively neutralized by the artillery.

10. Action on the objective. – Tanks, on arrival on the objective, will patrol their sectors to neutralize enemy weapons. In some cases the presence of the tanks on the objective will be sufficient to enable the infantry to secure it. Tanks must, however, always be prepared to deal with areas beyond or to the flank of their objectives if such action is necessary to assist the infantry. Patrols will be carried out so as to keep the tanks as far as possible "hull down" to enemy weapons beyond the objective. They will then hoist the all clear signal. They must not be left alone on the objective longer than necessary as this involves the danger of the enemy destroying them by artillery fire or by anti-tank guns moved forward, with a consequent risk of the enemy re-establishing themselves on the objective.

Liaison beforehand should have arranged a point where the senior tank company or section commander on the objective will meet the infantry battalion or company commander and ascertain that the infantry are up and that tanks can rally.

Tanks will in the first instance rally by sections under cover, if possible just in rear of the captured position. If the attack is to proceed to a further objective, they will deploy to resume the attack from these forward rallying points. On the final objective they will rally well back once the infantry notify that they are organized against counter-attack by both enemy infantry and A.F.Vs.

11. Maintenance of the momentum of the attack.- Once the organized resistance of the enemy is broken and the timed artillery program has ended, the further progress of this attack will depend on the initiative of forward units or sub-unit commanders

With tanks available it may be possible to achieve considerable success by means of rapidly mounted local attacks to defeat enemy elements still holding out.

In these circumstances decentralization will produce the quickest results and tank company commanders should operate under the orders of leading infantry unit commanders at this stage when speed and initiative are essential to success.'

As can be seen from these quotes the plan for a tank/infantry attack was for the greater part of the tanks to advance in front of the infantry who would follow at the rear of the tanks. The leading tanks would find safety in moving quickly to take advantage of the effects of the artillery, the following tanks would co-operate with the infantry.

Interestingly a similar type of formation was tried in an exercise reported in the German manual of 1927 referred to earlier (Chapter 3, Note 2), but in this case the observer, who may have been mistaken, seems to have regarded the leading tanks as a modern 'forlorn hope'.

'An alternative to the above scheme would allow the tanks to start from a greater distance away from their objective. In this they would attack in two waves. The first wave would try to crash through the enemy's front, this would force the enemy to concentrate on it. The second wave would, as

before, arrive at the front of the enemy's defensive zone with the infantry.

This plan makes best use of the high speed of the tanks, and may make a pursuit possible. However it appears to require a higher level of training, and could resulting heavier casualties.'

The Infantry tank action at Arras in 1940, described in the next chapter, must have seemed to confirm the effectiveness of tanks forging ahead of their infantry. This action, though, was more in the form of a meeting engagement than an assault on a field position, and although the tanks involved could make light of the German 37-mm AT guns, the baleful consequence of charging 88s seems to have been missed. Consequently the basic concept was exaggerated in subsequent manuals, and the policy became to require an advanced echelon of tanks up to 1,000 yards in front of the infantry with an echelon just in front, and a reserve just behind, the infantry.

This concept, so fine while Matilda II was Queen of the Battlefield, was to lead to disaster in Operation Battleaxe. The manual quoted below, 'The Infantry Division in the Attack'[2] was published in July 1941, the month after Battleaxe. This manual was reprinted, in Canada, in September 1941, which was a disgrace by any standards.

'8 Co-operation between army tanks and infantry
vii. Tank action.- The number of echelons of tanks, their tasks, and their position in relation to the infantry, will depend on the strength of the enemy, the ground, and the nature of any tank and infantry obstacles. Different phases of the same attack will often demand different formations.

The foremost localities are likely to be protected by wire, and covered extensively by a deep belt of fire from automatic weapons capable of being laid on fixed lines

38

from defiladed positions in depth. These positions must be neutralized, and the wire cut, before the infantry can advance without heavy casualties.

Against such resistance the formation of the advance will often be as follows:-

First echelon of tanks - Its task will be the neutralization of enemy defences in depth. It will move at best tank speed, engaging the enemy when found, particularly his anti-tank weapons. The object of this echelon will be to get on to the objective as quickly as possible, and it must not attempt to mop up the area crossed.

The first echelon may operate up to a maximum of 1,000 yards ahead of the leading infantry, but it should not completely out-run their support unless the opposition has been crushed.

When the attack reaches the enemy gun area, the leading echelon of tanks will probably work in close co-operation with the infantry in the manner suggested below for the second echelon during the earlier stages of the battle. This will reduce the chances of tanks suffering heavy casualties through coming unexpectedly upon field artillery sited to destroy them.

Second echelon of tanks.- Its task is the close support of the leading infantry, which it will provide by breaking passages through the wire and by neutralizing small arms fire from the foremost localities and from positions not dealt with by the first echelon.

The infantry will move at best infantry speed, which must govern the general rate of advance. So long as they are available to support the infantry when needed, the tanks should be free to move at top speed while actually engaging the enemy, thus presenting the least favourable targets to enemy anti-tank weapons.

The tanks of this echelon will move sometimes ahead of, and sometimes behind, the infantry they are supporting, as the opposition, ground, and cover may dictate. They must on no account cruise slowly along in front of the infantry, as by doing so they present the easiest of targets.

Third echelon of tanks.- This will consist of local reserves to deal with unexpected resistance in front or to a flank.

The object of these sub-units will be to help on infantry which have been held up. They must not be used to reinforce tanks which have failed to advance.

Fourth echelon of tanks.- This is the reserve of tanks which is retained to exploit success, and to deal with the unexpected counter-attack.'

Notes:
1) Tactical Handling of Army Tank Battalions, Military Training Pamphlet No 22, part III, Employment. 1939
2) Operations, Military Training Pamphlet No 23. Part IX.- The Infantry Division in the Attack. 1941

Chapter 5: Infantry Tanks in Action

Throughout the Second World War there were two distinct trends in the evolution of the use of Infantry Tanks. These trends were not shown during the first two years of the war when attacks were led by independent echelons of Infantry Tanks, tasks for which Cruiser Tanks were not suitable. However as the war progressed and AT weapons improved, so in such attacks these tactics became suicidal and were finally discarded.

After this it was seen that when supporting infantry attacking what manuals termed 'Hastily Organised Defences', or attacking troops that were not dug in at all, then the Infantry Tanks came to be used more and more as Cruisers would be. In Normandy there were never enough Infantry Tanks and many Cruisers were used for infantry support, and it was found that by 1945 there was no difference in the tactical use of the two types of tank.

Conversely for attacks against stronger defences, particularly those covered by minefields, the Infantry Tanks were largely replaced by specialised armour, and were reduced to providing escorts for these vulnerable vehicles.

The first evolutionary route mentioned here will be considered and illustrated in this chapter, the second in subsequent chapters.

1st Army Tank Brigade in France in 1940

This brigade was commanded by Brigadier Pratt and consisted of three Battalions: 4RTR, commanded by Lt-Col Fitzmaurice, 7RTR, Lt-Col Heyland and 8RTR which did not join the brigade due to shortage of tanks. The establishment of these battalions was 50 'I' tanks, seven light tanks and eight (Bren gun) carriers. As the establishment assumed fifty 2-pdrs, it must have been assumed that the Matilda I's would soon be replaced by Matilda II's.

The first troopships of the BEF left for France on 9th September. The infantry divisions went first, then 4RTR. 7RTR was still awaiting its tanks. 4RTR was up to establishment, but only with Matilda I's. It spent the winter at Domart, close to the Somme.

When the brigade was first deployed a study drawn up to consider its use concluded that, because the Matilda I's lacked an AT gun, they could only be used to defend static AT guns against infantry assault. This should be in an anti-tank defence zone behind the front line.
The study's conclusion was that until the Matilda II's were issued, the contribution of the Army Tank Brigade was limited. This comment may be taken as something of a criticism of the general who drew up the specification for the Matilda I.

7RTR arrived in early May 1940. On 10th May the German offensive started. 7RTR had 27 Matilda I's, 23 Matilda II's, and seven light tanks. Some of the Matilda I's had been upgunned to mount .5-in MGs.

The two battalions would have had no time to exercise together when, in response to the German attack, Plan 'D' was activated and the BEF trundled forward to take up its position on the Dyle. The tanks were sent by rail, admin vehicles by road, and arrived at the railhead at Halle during the night of 14th/15th May. Next night the brigade took up a position in the Forest of Soignies. This move of the BEF fell in with the German plans and they mounted a major attack in the Sedan area and crossed the Meuse on 13th May. Then, with seven panzer divisions, they surged due west towards the Channel.

The result was a long salient, 20 to 30 miles wide. On the map it was very vulnerable to an Allied counter-attack which, even if only partly successful, would have choked off supplies for the German tanks. The Germans were well aware of this and their infantry divisions were hard at work widening the breach. To make this counter-attack the 1st Army Tank Brigade was ordered to Tournai. The tanks should have been entrained at Enghien, but as a result of air attacks there were no trains available, so the tanks had to drive on their tracks, mostly at around 3 mph, the whole way.

British plans evolved at two levels. On the higher level the plan was to take advantage of the opportunity offered by the enemy salient and counter-attacks were proposed, a French one from the south and a British one from the north. However on a local level the plan was for a spoiling attack designed to interrupt German communications and assist the defence of Arras. Initially the plan was for two divisions to be involved, but circumstances whittled this down to one brigade, which could only put two battalions into the assault, and the 1st Army Tank Brigade. The French attack was not a success, but even so the limited success of the British attack made a surprising impression on the German command and is a hint of what could have been achieved in slightly more favourable circumstances.

The attacking force was to be commanded by Major-General Martel who commanded the 50th Division which supplied the infantry component of one brigade. The force was organised into two columns, the term 'battle groups' was not yet current. Each column was a battalion of infantry and a battalion of tanks with artillery attached. 7RTR with 8DLI were the right, or western, column; 4RTR with 6DLI were the left, or eastern, column. The Tank Brigade having moved on its tracks around 120 miles since leaving the railhead, had lost a considerable number of tanks. It was down to 58 Matilda I's and 16 Matilda II's. To equalise firepower seven Madilda II's, with crews, were lent by 7RTR to 4RTR.

The brigade was ordered to form up behind, north of, the Arras-Doullens road. This road ran roughly south-west from Arras and looked like a good start line on the map, but the Germans were already north of it, having troops on the Arras-Hesdin road, which ran west-north-west from Arras. It is not known why this information was apparently ignored, perhaps British staff procedures were still geared to trench warfare speed. Aerial reconnaissance also let the army down. In particular this may have been because the RAF was returning to England while this action was afoot. Even so the whole campaign was carried out in the face of German aerial superiority, a fact disconcerting for British morale.

The aim was for the two columns, which would be operating about two miles apart, to make a 180 degree sweep round the south of Arras, and finish up by taking up a position on the Scarpe to its east. The orders were passed on to the battalions at 7.30 am. Unfortunately it was not defined which of the two battalion commanders should command each column. This would cause problems not helped by the poor radio communications of the time. A French tank unit of around 60 tanks was to co-operate on the right flank, and the French insisted that the start line was changed to the Arras-Hesdin road. This was to be crossed at 2.0 pm. The tanks had to cover nearly eight miles to reach it, and the infantry had to march that distance. General Martel followed the attacking columns in a staff car but it does not appear that he was able to influence the course of the action. Also totally out of contact with the tanks was Brigadier Pratt. He was visited close to the start line by Brigadier Pope, who was the Adviser on Armoured Fighting Vehicles at HQ, BEF. Pope urged him forward to his brigade, but it is not obvious what he could have done when he got there.

There was certainly no shortage of chiefs, but without radios they could achieve little.

Remarkably, one tank commander had not yet sloughed off his peacetime habits and halted at a level crossing barrier. Another tank, with a more resolute commander, rolled past him and smashed through it.

In the event the attack started half-an-hour late, and then not all the troops had closed up. Before crossing the start line the troops had to cover three miles and cross the Scarpe, where there were still bridges standing. Then they were in action.

It was a great misfortune that in the haste to get started there was no time for reconnaissance. Each column should have had a motorcycle platoon provided for short-range reconnaissance but the right hand column did not receive theirs. So they only found out about the enemy when they opened fire. This they did at the village of Duisans which was cleared by the DLI and some French tanks. The 8DLI continued on but were stopped by mortar fire before reaching the Arras-Doulens road. 7RTR drove on without them

Soon after crossing the start line a troop of the right hand company (squadron) shot up a German AT unit in half-tracks. This unit must have been a flank guard for an infantry unit of the 7th Panzer Division or the SS Totenkopf Division, for, as the rest of the battalion breasted a small rise they could see a large number of lorries full of infantry crossing their front to their right. The MGs on the tanks opened up, causing heavy casualties. The Germans got some 37-mm AT guns into action, but their shot bounced harmlessly off the thick armour of the Matildas of which one of the Mk IIs absorbed 14 hits with equinamity. Some of the German troops showed signs of panic.

German dive bombers were commendably quickly on the scene, and were effective against the infantry, but only destroyed two tanks. In one case bombs bursting close to a Matilda I turned it over, killing the commander, in another a light tank was blown into the air. Brigadier Pratt wrote that it was believed that it was actually blown 15 feet in the air!

4RTR fought its way through to Wancourt, causing havoc, but then it ran into the German field batteries, following their infantry. The result was tragic. The Colonel, who had been commanding from a light tank because of the better radio, was killed and around 20 tanks were knocked out. The adjutant led a charge that destroyed one battery, but there were others and he had to order the battalion to pull back.

Partly as a result of the tanks' charge the infantry of 6DLI had been left well behind by 4RTR. They were slowed down by mopping up and collecting prisoners, and in terms of practical co operation, had lost contact with the tanks.

7RTR had not only cast off from its infantry but took a different direction. It should have been making for Warlus, but swung towards Wailly. At this moment communications within the battalion failed. The Colonel dismounted from his light tank to try, by hand signals, to restore order and direction but he was killed by MG fire, as was his adjutant who bravely tried to carry on for him. 7RTR tanks rumbled into Wailly and Mercatel and caused great destruction, but by that time General Rommel, who commanded the 7th Panzer Division, had returned from the division's spearhead to the west to direct the defence against the two tank battalions.

He set about deploying various artillery pieces, most notably some 88-mm guns, to build up what was later termed a '*pakfront*'. If the tanks could not charge artillery and machine gun the crews they were helpless, not being able to fire high explosives, and the infantry could not tackle the German guns having been left far behind. 7RTR was forced to retreat.

This was really the end of the part played by the British tanks in this action. They pulled back over the Scarpe. There were only two Matilda II's and 26 Matilda I's left. A small number of damaged tanks was salvaged, but the bulk had to be abandoned. Some German tanks joined in the fray, but found that their guns could not defeat the Matildas' armour, whereas the 2-pdrs were very effective against German armour.

Fortunately the German follow-up was hindered, not only by the chaos of the battlefield but also by British infantry units holding villages, and AT guns that scored many successes against the German tanks. The Germans quickly learned not to charge AT batteries. They also learned that they would need thicker armour on their tanks and soon set about a program of bolting extra plates on the fronts of them. They had lost 400 men as prisoners and around 20 tanks.

This action is justly celebrated in the history of the RTR and is often stated as the cause of the halt order that allowed the BEF to escape at Dunkirk. That view might be something of an exaggeration but the action certainly made a significant impression on the German command. As Field Marshal von Rundstedt later commented: '*A critical moment in the drive came just as my forces had reached the Channel. It was caused by a British counter-stroke southwards from Arras. For a short time, it was feared that the Panzer divisions would be cut off.*'

It is no exaggeration to say that the 1st Army Tank Brigade was destroyed as a result of this action. After Arras, reorganised as a regiment, it carried out only small and unimportant actions until the last two surviving tanks were disabled by their crews at Dunkirk.

Operation Compass

In 1940 an Italian army invaded Egypt. This invasion was a slow and stately affair, the Italians covered 60 miles in four days, then halted and constructed a series of five major fortified camps and four smaller ones, stretching south into the desert from the two coastal positions of Sidi Barrani and Maktila. These fortifications formed a screen which, when the decision was taken to repel the invasion, the 7th Armoured Division would penetrate before thundering off in the direction of Sollum. Inevitably the capture of these camps was a necessary part of the action. It was carried out by the 4th Indian Division, spearheaded by the 'I' tanks of 7RTR, now all Matilda IIs, the action of the 'I' tanks perfectly complementing that of the Armoured Division's Cruisers.

The most important capture was Nibeiwa. Not only was this the closest to the route of the 7th Armoured Division, but it contained the Maletti Group, which approximated to a small armoured division, so could have been a threat to the 7th Armoured Division's communications. It was a large site surrounded by a stone wall and an AT ditch, between these was a minefield. The ditch was nowhere near as formidable as aerial photographs made it look, but the mines were. That mines could be a major threat to 'I' tanks had been appreciated, and attempts had been made to produce a mine plough to be carried on the Matilda I. Unfortunately these ploughs had not gone into production so the tanks just had to be careful not to stray into the minefield.

General O'Connor held an exercise which was a rehearsal for the assault, the troops attacking a position of the same shape and size as Nibeiwa. As security was a major problem the possible target of the real assault was kept hidden. The exercise was run along the lines laid down by the relevant manual, 'The Division in the Attack', which has already been extensively quoted. It was found that this approach would require the tanks to wait at the forming up place for two hours while the artillery registered its guns and commenced the bombardment. They would then advance in three echelons. The leading echelon would be on the objective at least twenty minutes before the arrival of the second with the infantry. The third echelon would follow as a reserve.

The assault on Nibeiwa had to proceed faster. The artillery was not required to destroy the enemy, but to keep his head down. The tanks would go straight in, if they could get among the enemy they would cause the necessary destruction. The infantry would follow, staying in their lorries until the last moment. The plan depended on the knowledge that the Italians had no weapons that could penetrate the Matilda's armour, but even so it could only work if total surprise could be achieved.

The move forward had to be carried out exactly to plan. Infantry tanks move slowly anyway, but to ensure minimum track wear the regimental commander, Colonel Jerram, decreed that they should not be driven faster than half their top speed, that is at 7mph, consequently their advance started well before the rest of the attacking force. They took two days to cover 60 miles then laid up for 24 hours within five miles of Nibeiwa for rest and maintenance. They were joined here by their infantry. Only during the move forward were the crews told it was not just an exercise but the real thing.

While the tanks were on the move reconnaissance units had discovered that the AT ditch and minefield did not extend completely round the Italian camp, but there was a considerable area to the west with neither. This was where the main entrance was, and was, naturally, the side furthest away from the British. This was obviously where the assault would have to take place.

To have advanced this far and to have got so close to the Italians without being seen was a great achievement, but they could be discovered at any time so the attack had to go in the next morning, 9th December 1940. To keep the Italians occupied and to drown out the noise of the tanks the camp was bombed overnight. An infantry battalion approached the camp from the north-east and at dawn opened up a heavy, but presumably not very deadly, fire. Then the artillery opened up.

While the Italians were distracted by all this, 7RTR and the infantry battalion formed up close to the gap in the AT ditch and minefield. Because of the comparative narrowness of the gap the attacking squadron could only attack on a two troop front, each troop having two tanks forward. Some of the tanks carried fascines for crossing the AT ditch, but it turned out that aerial photography had exaggerated the size of this obstacle and the fascines were not needed.

What the reconnaissance had failed to discover was that it was the Italian procedure to station 22 tanks in the gap overnight. Their crews were either sleeping or totally relaxed and were caught entirely by surprise by the British tanks. It seems extraordinary that the diversionary small arms fire and artillery had been ignored by these crewmen, also tank units in such positions would be expected to move out before dawn and take up battle positions as a standard precautionary measure. The Italian tanks did not stand a chance. Their crews were mostly machine gunned on their feet. Some bravely tried to mount up but their tanks were shot through easily by the British 2-pdrs. All 22 tanks were knocked out with no loss to the British.

The British attacked with only one squadron. Some of the tanks entered the camp through the main gate, some crashed through the stone wall. Once they were on the inside of the camp they could set about machine gunning the garrison. Some of the defenders surrendered immediately, some put up a valiant, if doomed, resistance. There were several cases of Italian soldiers attacking tanks with grenades. Most notably the Italian artillery fought back. Only their AA guns could damage the tanks, and several tanks had their turrets jammed by strikes at the turret bases close to the race. This, naturally, rendered the tanks almost useless, their only armament being in the turret. Only one tank was actually knocked out. That happened when the driver opened the cover to his direct vision block. He did that at just the wrong moment. A 20-mm round entered, killed him and, ricocheting around wounded the rest of the crew. The greatest loss suffered by the squadron was that of the squadron leader who was shot when he dismounted to inspect damage to his tank, probably caused by a mine.

The infantry follow-up was impressive. The battalion, preceded by 'B' squadron, stayed on its lorries to within 200 yards of the main gate. The troops then dismounted and surged towards it. They were met by heavy small arms (SA) fire and sustained several casualties, but finally fought their way in to accept many surrenders.

As soon as it was plain that resistance had ended 'B' squadron was left with the infantry as a defence against counter-attack, 'A' squadron and the remainder of the regiment proceeded to the rallying point to the north of Nibeiwa. Unfortunately *en route* five tanks were disabled when they ran over mines. Once at the rallying point the jammed turrets were freed and the tanks replenished with fuel and ammunition. Then the tanks, accompanied by a different battalion, trundled off northwards to attack Tummar West. The major problem was finding that camp as a dust storm blew up and the tanks had to approach it on a compass bearing. Once here the assault went in as it had done at Nibeiwa. Some Italians, particularly the artillery, fought gallantly, but they were helpless against the Matildas, and resistance soon ceased.

At this point the infantry brigade commander, probably worried by the large number of prisoners his men had to guard, insisted on retaining the bulk of the tanks in case of counter-attacks. This left only nine tanks available for further assaults. This figure included two repaired mine casualties from Nibeiwa that had come up after the fall of Tummar West. These tanks set off and, having more than their share of luck, captured Tummars East and Central. Tummar East was very undermanned as most of the garrison was away planning a counter-attack on Nibeiwa.

With the fall of the Tummars the pattern had been established so that, once Matildas were within a position's perimeter, that position could be regarded as lost. Sidi Barrani, Bardia and Tobruk were to fall in turn and the only remaining factor seemed to be that the Matildas had to move from one triumph to the next on their tracks. It was only a pity that tank transporters had not been provided. Nevertheless the campaign against the Italians had shown Matilda II to be the Queen of the Battlefield. The Germans would depose her.

Operation Battleaxe

Following Operation Compass there was a substantial redeployment of British forces, mostly occasioned by the Greek campaign, that coincided with the arrival of General Rommel and the Afrika Korps, and that resulted in the British troops, except for the Tobruk garrison, being driven back to Egypt.

The situation for the forces in Egypt was difficult and, at what at the time seemed a great risk, the Tiger convoy carrying tanks and aircraft, was sent out from the UK. After the convoy's arrival considerable political pressure was put on General Wavell to open an offensive, to be called Operation Battleaxe, to destroy Rommel's forces and relieve Tobruk. Even despite Tiger, Wavell's forces were not that large.

The British Troops
The principal units were:
Western Desert Force, Commander Lieutenant General Sir Noel Beresford-Pierse

7th Armoured Division – Maj Gen M O'M Creagh
    4th Armoured Brigade – Brigadier A Gatehouse
        4RTR – Lt Col W O'Carroll, 44 Matilda IIs
        7RTR – Lt Col B Groves, 48 Matilda IIs
    7th Armoured Brigade – Brigadier H E Russell
        Two Cruiser regiments
    Support Group – Brigadier J Campbell
        A regiment of RHA – sixteen 25-pdrs
        An AT battery – twelve 2-pdrs *portees*
        Two battalions
4th Indian Division – Maj Gen FW Messervy
    11th Indian Brigade
    22nd Guards Brigade

As can be seen both divisions were under strength, but both the 4th Armoured Brigade regiments were up to strength, thanks to the Tiger convoy. In addition to the Matildas they each had six light tanks and two Cruisers for command and control. 7RTR had a squadron in Tobruk, but this had been replaced by a squadron made up from 5RTR which had yet to receive all its tanks.

The Axis forces that had to be defeated in the first part of the operation included two German panzer divisions, one in the frontier zone, one in reserve close to Tobruk. There was a weak Italian infantry division at Bardia and three battalions, with artillery, in the Sollum – Capuzzo area. A number of locations, such as Halfaya, Point 206 and Hafid Ridge, were fortified and garrisoned with German and Italian troops. The British were generally well informed of all this, except for details of the fortified positions.

The British did not enter this action lightly. An earlier operation, 'Brevity', had been called off when it was found that the Germans were stronger than expected. The only gain had been the Halfaya Pass, but this was soon lost again to the Germans. General Wavell was less than confident about Operation Battleaxe, he fully appreciated the vulnerability of the Matildas to the larger calibre German AT guns, and considered these tanks too slow for desert fighting.

The plan, in terms of armour, was for the Cruisers of 7th Armoured Brigade to be deployed on the desert, western, flank. It was to cover the open flank of the 4th Indian Division, and destroy any German armour in the Hafid Ridge area. 4th Armoured Brigade was to come directly under the 4th Indian Division for the first part of the operation. 4RTR was to provide one-and-a-half squadrons (18 'I' tanks) to support the Indian Brigade in its assault on the Halfaya Pass. The remainder of the brigade, supported by the Guards Brigade, was to attack between the other two forces to capture Point 206 and Capuzzo. It would then threaten Bardia, Sollum and the rear of the German positions at Halfaya. It was then expected to rejoin 7th Armoured Division for a final tank battle in the desert.

The approach march commenced on 14th June 1941 and continued overnight, the total advance was 32 miles. The first action undertaken was the right hand column's assault on Halfaya Pass, supported by six of the 4RTR tanks. Unfortunately the tanks ran into a minefield where four were immobilised, and although these tanks continued to give fire support for the infantry, the attack stalled.

The other squadron attacked on higher ground above the escarpment. The tanks moved forward slowly so as to make the minimum noise, and deployed into two lines in front of an infantry battalion at 5.40 am. They then waited for covering fire from their supporting battery of 25-pdrs. This fire did not come, the battery, being wheeled, had bogged down in soft sand that the tanks and infantry had been able to cross. At 6.00, having heard the right hand assault in action, the tanks attacked without artillery support. The Germans had dug in four 88s, eight 2-cm AA guns and eight Italian 100-mm howitzers of Great War vintage. One 88 was move down to oppose the coastal column, but the remaining three destroyed the squadron, cold bloodedly holding their fire until the tanks were within 300 metres. The tanks did not go charging in as was sometimes the later fashion for British armour, but advanced carefully, trying to edge round to their left to outflank the Germans. It did no good, by midday there was only one Matilda and a light tank left. The infantry assault has halted in it tracks.

This action is usually taken as a turning point in the career of Matilda II. After the action, while touring the battlefield close to Halfaya with General Rommel, his aide, Lieutenant Schmidt, heard a captured British tank driver, who was probably too used to thinking in terms of the ineffective 37-mm AT guns at Arras, say, with reference to an 88, '*it is unfair to use flak against our tanks*'. A German artilleryman, hearing this translated, replied '*Yes, and I think it is most unfair of you to attack with tanks whose armour nothing but an 88 will penetrate*'.

The 7th Armoured Brigade ran into trouble at Hafid Ridge. British tactical reconnaissance had been functioning badly due to its armoured cars being outclassed by the heavier German ones, and because German aircraft had taken to attacking them. Consequently they had no idea of the German field fortifications that were waiting for them, and which stopped their progress.

The centre column started off at 10.30 am. 4RTR was cover the left flank and capture Point 206 and 7RTR at Capuzzo. 4RTR led with 'A' Squadron, but without any accompanying infantry. This squadron had provided the two troops in action on the coast. The Squadron Leader with two troops overran a small post, BP38, on the frontier wire while the remaining troop had peeled off heading for point 206.

Point 206 was rather stronger than was expected, containing an infantry company, eight 105-mm guns, three 37-mm and three 50-mm AT guns and two 20-mm AA guns. The troop heading for it was destroyed, one tank falling out due to mechanical problems, the other two being hit by AT fire. The Squadron Leader then came back to make a personal reconnaissance but his tank and an accompanying one were knocked out.

While the Squadron Leader's attention was fixed on Point 206 some German armoured cars attacked the troop at BP38, capturing three tanks and the troops he had left there. The Germans were driven away by artillery fire, but it was plain that the requirement was for infantry. Consequently a company of Guards was instructed to RV with the tanks close to BP38. Before they came the Squadron Leader attacked point 206 again with all available tanks, four. They were reduced to one, and that one was driven off.

This last assault seems pointless, but the communications of the time were not good and he might have been unaware that an infantry company was trying to find him. His requests for 'B' Squadron to join in the attack were refused by General Messervy, who presumably was worried, until late in the day, about the possibility of a counter-attack but then the sixteen tanks of 'B' Squadron, well supported by artillery and an infantry company, captured the post, but only after the last AT gun had been knocked out.

7RTR's objective was Capuzzo. Remarkably it formed up at 11.00 am close to point 206, which might have resulted in the garrison of that place thinking that they had repelled more attacks than was the case, but it does not seem that they shot at 7RTR.

Capuzzo had a garrison of a company of Italian infantry with two 37-mm AT guns, which could be effective against Cruisers, but not Matildas. Perhaps its easy capture was anticipated by the Germans because they moved up a panzer regiment for a counter-attack, and deployed four 88s to its west to take attacking tanks in their flanks.

7RTR attacked at 1.30 pm with two squadrons forward. Not surprisingly the sight of around thirty Matildas was too much for the defenders who pulled out. Five tanks of the left hand squadron were knocked out by the 88s. The first of several counter-attacks was beaten off before 4.0 pm when the Colonel reported to Brigade that his tanks were on the objective. The infantry, escorted by the third squadron, arrived at 5.30 pm, but it took some time to make the area secure, and the tanks did not pull out to rally to the south of Capuzzo until 9.30 pm. By then there were only seventeen left.

At the end of the first day although there had been some undeniable disappointments, the central column had done well and, if its 'I' tanks could be returned to 7th Armoured Division and used to destroy the fieldworks behind Hafid Ridge, the operation could still be a success.

Such optimism would seem to ignore the Germans. Next day counter-attacks prevented the release of 4th Armoured Brigade even though the Guards Brigade was now dug in at

Capuzzo. The action was fierce and German tanks suffered heavy casualties, 50 out of 80 being immobilised. They had to come to close range to penetrate the Matildas' armour, but this brought them to ranges where the 2-pdrs were effective, hence their heavy casualties.

Elsewhere, throughout the morning the Indian Brigade kept hammering away at the Halfaya Pass, but with negligible tank support it was not successful. The 7th Armoured Brigade fought on, generally inconclusively, at Hafid Ridge. Late evening a German counter-attack got under way that would go as far as Sidi Suleiman then swing towards Halfaya. This endangered the British forces which were then pulled back. That really concluded the operation. The Matildas functioned well escorting the Guards Brigade to the rear.

The intense driving spirit of the German pursuit was illustrated by the loss of one Matilda that was actually rammed by a German command tank that had only a wooden imitation main armament.

Operation Battleaxe was a failure, particularly from the point of view of the 'I' tanks. Of roughly 90 tanks which started the operation, 64 were lost and abandoned. Matilda was no longer Queen of the Battlefield. Attention is usually drawn to the squadron being massacred by the AT guns at Halfaya, giving the impression that the tanks advanced in a wild charge. This was not the case. These were highly experienced troops and presumably not suicidal. The Germans had had time to dig their guns in, hidden from observation and with fields of fire designed to strike the thinner side armour of the Matildas. Tanks attacking in such circumstances could only hope for success if they had heavy artillery support, but there were no guns, and the morning mist would have made observation difficult.

The central column was almost a success. Perhaps if a less ambitious, step by step, role had been planned, and if the infantry and artillery could have kept up, it could have captured Sollum, freeing the Halfaya Pass. While this was happening the 7th Armoured Brigade would have had to adopt a defensive stance, but it is hard to imaging that Rommel would have outflanked it knowing that it was untouched and ready to outflank him. Perhaps then, after a short pause, a tank battle could have been sought and the march to Tobruk begun.

Operation Battleaxe has been treated by history as a fairly minor and unimportant British defeat, but it should be remembered at least for the superb *Rommelei* of the breakthrough to Sidi Suleiman, and the way this breakthrough might have paved the way to the disastrous 'dash to the wire', which was an important action in the 'Crusader' battle.

However perhaps the most significant aspect of Battleaxe was that it represented the nadir of infantry/tank co-operation. There were two problems. The first was that the accepted procedure for the deployment of Infantry Tanks was flawed. The procedure called for the first wave of tanks to be independent of infantry and to be on the objective half-an-hour before the infantry follow-up. This system could only work against a reasonable opposition if the artillery support was overwhelming. It worked in Operation Compass because at Nibeiwa the attacking troops achieved total surprise, the defenders had minimal AT weapons and the infantry follow-up was enthusiastic. In subsequent actions the Italians became progressively demoralised and unwilling to fight against 'I' tanks.

The second problem was that even these poor tactics might have worked if they had been applied, but in Battleaxe the artillery support was poor – non-existent at Halfaya – and the infantry were totally disconnected from the tanks. This was partly the result of the offensive being mounted in a rush, and partly the result of extensive personnel changes. A few large scale exercises should have improved things.

The Normandy Campaign

The climactic experience for the British army, and also for 'I' tanks, was the Normandy Campaign. However the effectiveness of 'I' tank units was difficult to judge and complicated by two main factors. One was that there were plenty of other tanks involved, Shermans and Cromwells. They were in three British armoured divisions, and Canadian and Polish divisions, on the British front alone. Also there were five independent armoured brigades with Shermans, one was Canadian and one was disbanded shortly after 'D' day, and three tank brigades with Churchills. The difference between the two kinds of brigade was that the tank brigades had no organic infantry, whereas armoured brigades did. As far as infantry support went there seems to have been no difference in the deployment of the two types of brigade. Field Marshal Montgomery much preferred armoured brigades to tank brigades because of the greater flexibility in their use. They could replace armoured brigades in armoured divisions if casualties made this necessary, but tank brigades, having no motor battalion, could not function in armoured divisions.

Despite Operation Goodwood, and a small number of other operations, the bulk of the use tanks were put to in Normandy was infantry support, which is the subject of this study, but how this support was provided does not fall easily into a general pattern, either for Sherman or Churchill units.

The salient fact about the Normandy campaign is that since Dunkirk the British Army had had nothing to do but prepare for it, and while it had been preparing other units of the army had been fighting, mostly in North Africa. This meant that its training manuals could be continually checked against reality, so its training would be up-to-date, but, sadly, as far as infantry support went this trend was not achieved.

As has been seen the training undertaken after Dunkirk for infantry assaults supported by Infantry Tanks required the first echelon of tanks to advance in front of the infantry. Probably the necessity of training in open areas, like Salisbury Plain, resulted in such procedures lingering on longer than they should have. However reports of the vulnerability of tanks unaccompanied by infantry began to be received and a steady evolution of tactics started which moved the leading tanks back closer to the infantry, then actually behind them. This evolution led to an ideal of a tank squadron of five troops supporting the three attacking platoons of an infantry company. One troop would support each platoon, following along behind it. The other two troops were available, if required, to move out to a flank to provide remote fire support, or to replace casualties or thicken the firing line. This was the standard deployment for Churchill tanks that was being phased in when Field Marshall Montgomery took over command of the 21st Army Group in early 1944. Unfortunately he insisted in replacing it with 8th Army practice which had the tanks take over the lead after the outer crust of the AT defences had been penetrated. This was the procedure that the troops took to Normandy. However, by and large British infantry support worked well. This was at least partly due to commanders on the ground being prepared to ignore the manuals and apply common sense.

Infantry support operations were always going to be difficult in close country like the bocage. The most significant problem was the difficulty the infantry had in communicating with tank commanders. It is true that the infantry had radios that should have made communications possible but in practice they very seldom actually worked. German infantrymen were told to deliberately target radiomen. However when the radios could be made to work the results were good. In addition each tank carried at its stern an infantry/tank telephone. This was a field telephone, and pressing a bar on the hand set sent a loud 'beep' through the crew's headsets, so it could hardly be ignored. The obvious disadvantage was that, for the infantryman, using this telephone within range of the Germans was apt to be suicidal, and out of range it was unnecessary.

The best procedure was through an 'O' group held shortly before the action, in which every possibility could be considered. There were two disadvantages. One was that it is impossible to consider every possibility as so many depended on the enemy. Secondly it was not always possible to hold a lengthy 'O' group. In many cases the tanks and infantry only linked up a short time before the action was due to start.

Communications were necessary for the infantry to indicate targets to the tanks. The system would break down because the tanks and infantry would advance at different rates. The tanks would be slowed right down by bocage hedgerows, swamps and mines; the infantry by SA fire.

It was often the case that the infantry was quite happy to be some distance away from the tanks. Tanks in motion are impossible to camouflage, in fact they advertise their presence, and they attract a good deal of fire, so the infantry were glad not to be too close. Also if a tank were hit and burned, as Shermans tended to, the Germans would often shell it, providing another reason for the infantry to dislike tanks.

The drill-like procedure for infantry support, with the tanks advancing line abreast might work well on Salisbury Plain but in Normandy it just did not work, at least partly because the Germans only dug in to defend places where classic tactics would not work, so force of circumstance made the tanks advance in groups, which did have the advantage of enabling the concentration of their firepower. This trend was more pronounced with Sherman regiments than with Churchill regiments. Montgomery refused to make a distinction between the two types of regiment. Some Sherman regiments found that they could support the infantry more effectively by deploying in larger units, squadrons at least, remotely from the infantry usually to a flank, and applying fire and movement.

As mine warfare increased in importance so did the need for the flails of specialised armour. The role of Infantry Tanks came to be to provide fire support for these vehicles, which were very vulnerable to AT guns, then, secondarily, to support the infantry who might be in APCs. This will be considered in Chapter 7.

Once the infantry was on its objective, it was the duty of the tanks to stay with them to provide AT protection until the infantry AT guns could be moved up and emplaced. The Germans usually counter-attacked when a position had been lost, and if the tanks withdrew too soon the infantry's morale could be affected and the counter-attack could succeed. Unfortunately the tanks could be vulnerable during this period if the infantry commander would not allow them to pull back into hull down positions.

The Germans
The operations in North Africa since Alamein, and so far in Italy, had emphasised the importance of AT mines, but there were two other AT developments whose full importance was not yet appreciated. These were the Panzerfaust and the self-propelled AT gun. The former would make close country and urban areas even more dangerous for tanks, and the latter, having a bigger gun than the equivalent tank, could dominate open country.

No doubt if the Germans in Normandy had had the resources and the time they would have set up a deep zonal defence as they did in the Great War, but they were short of both. Consequently their field defences tended to consist of two belts of field fortifications. The Main Line of Resistance (*Hauptkampflinie*), and the Advanced Position (*Vorgeschobene Stellung*). The two lines were 4,000 to 6,000 yards apart. Between these lines (belts), were small fortified positions, as many as were appropriate to the terrain. It is important to note that, because of the units deployed between the two defensive belts, it would not be obvious to the attackers that he actually was between them.

The advanced position was manned by small units covering the obvious approaches, and artillery observers. The tasks of the troops were to keep out enemy patrols, force attacking units to deploy and provide warnings of enemy actions. Heavy weapons, particularly self-propelled AT guns would only be deployed in the Main Line of Resistance.

The 13th/18th Royal Hussars at La Bijude and Epron

Operation Charnwood was the major, and partly successful, assault on Caen. The ground action started early on 8th July 1944 after a huge bombing raid on the city. Among the first defences encountered by the British troops was a series of defended villages to the north of Caen. Among these were La Bijude and Epron which stood on the main road south to Caen. They were held by troops of the 12th SS Panzer Division Hitler Jugend and were to be attacked by the 176th Infantry Brigade of the 59th Division. The brigade, commanded by Brigadier Fryer, was to be supported by the Shermans of the 13th/18th Royal Hussars.

The 59th Division was a territorial division, and this was to be the first action of the 176th Brigade. The Hussars regarded the division as rather amateurish, but then the 13th/18th had already seen plenty of action. The 59th Division was disbanded the following month.

The Hussar's regimental HQ was close to the brigade HQ and the 7th South Staffordshire Regiment, the brigade reserve, in Le Mesnil wood. 'A' squadron, in reserve, stayed close to the regimental HQ. 'B' squadron was to be under the command of the 6th North Staffordshire Regiment in its attack on La Bijude. 'C' squadron was on the left, supporting 7th Norfolk Regiment attacking Epron. The first advance of the day was to be made by one company of each battalion. This meant a squadron supporting a company which, later in the campaign, came to be the preferred balance. The action was planned to proceed in two phases. Phase I was the attack on La Bijude which would be supported by both squadrons. For Phase II, 'C' squadron would rejoin the Norfolks and they would then attack Epron. *(See Sketch 2)*

The tanks formed up in battle formation at 2.0am, first light, with 'B' squadron and its infantry company to the west of the Chateau de la Londe, 'C' squadron and infantry to the east of the chateau . The Phase I attack jumped off at 4.20am, 20 minutes late. 'B' squadron's objective, the village of La Bijude, was 500 yards away, had already seen some heavy fighting and was largely ruined. The artillery preparation caused thick dust. Due to this dust and smoke 'B' squadron had difficulty in locating the German defences, in fact the Germans were entrenched to the west of the village. At 5.15 the squadron reported that they had taken the village, they had tanks on both sides of it and 'C' squadron on their left. Unfortunately the infantry, probably having been mortared, had gone to ground on the eastern side of the main road and could not be induced to enter the village. A possible reason for the infantry's reluctance to advance was the presence of German tanks, the sighting of one was reported by 'B' squadron at 5.45am, and its destruction a few minutes later. Nevertheless this meant that the tanks, now vulnerable to attack by the German infantry, also had to pull back.

By this time the location of the German position was known, and the infantry finally occupied La Bijude and dug in to its west, but it could be that they felt that their orders were to attack the village and not the field fortifications further on. However from their position the Germans could fire on the main road to Caen so they had to be moved. The German position included some dug-in tanks, and these knocked out two Shermans, fortunately without loss to the crews. By 12.40 the squadron could report that it had destroyed two Panzer IVs and three dug-in tanks that it described as 'being used as pillboxes'.

The Norfolks got the order to launch Phase II at 7.50am. They should have proceeded to La Bijude, joined 'C' squadron then marched on Epron, 600 yards away. It seems that, probably to stay clear of MG fire from La Bijude, they veered to the east. Whatever the case they did not join 'C' squadron as quickly as expected, and the tanks spent some time in an exposed position. While they were there a sergeant tank commander in 'C' squadron was killed when an artillery shell exploded on his turret, and another was wounded by a mortar bomb. When the company finally started to move the squadron leader's tank was knocked out by a panzerfaust. The soldier responsible was 'knocked out', presumably killed, by the squadron captain. Remarkably the squadron leader did not take over another tank but remained on foot to encourage the infantry along.

By this time the infantry radios were no longer working and the only communication the Norfolks had with brigade was via the tanks' radios. This was not that satisfactory for the tank commanders who found difficulty in contacting the infantry colonels whose messages were being received.

By 8.30 the Norfolks were reporting that they had reached the northern edge of Epron and were being supported by 'C' squadron. They had sustained serious casualties from fire from both flanks, their advance having been over open ground. At 1.0pm they reported that they had three platoons with three troops of 'C' squadron on the southern edge of Epron. This news, though welcome, was actually false but it took some time for this to be appreciated. At 6.0pm 'A' squadron was ordered to send a troop to join the reserve battalion, the South Staffords, and proceed to Epron. In the event this battalion could only provide one company for this task. The move was timed for 8.0pm. The tanks and infantry were to rendezvous at to the Norfolk Regiment's HQ at the Chateau de la Londe.

The squadron captain then proceeded to the chateau and found that a composite company, that is all the troops that were available, of the Norfolks were also to go to Epron. Their regimental HQ, like the brigade HQ, had been out of touch with their company in Epron since mid-morning, and thought that Epron was captured. The captain then proceeded to La Bijude and reported this situation to the CO, 13th/18th, and then to the Brigadier.

At 1.30pm an 'O' group was held on the road by La Bijude to plan the assault on the German position to the west of the village. It would be made by the South Staffords, less the company that was on its way to Epron. It was to be supported by flame-throwing tanks (Crocodiles) and flails and was expected to start at 5.0pm. At 5.0 it was postponed until 9.30pm.

At 7.45pm the two companies, one Norfolk, one South Staffords, and a troop of 'A' squadron were ready to move off from around La Bijude. The squadron leader insisted on a change of plan as originally it was presumed that the move was a simple reinforcement to troops in Epron, and it was now known not to be the case. Consequently 'C' squadron with the 'A' squadron troop poured some suppressive fire into Epron before the infantry went in. They reported the village as captured at 10.00pm having met negligible resistance and picked up 15 prisoners. The Germans had pulled out because the Luftwaffe Field Division to their right had retreated leaving them in a very exposed position. 'C' squadron put two troops either side of the village and the 'A' squadron troop reconnoitred south towards Caen until it came across an AT ditch dug across the road.

At 9.30pm the attack on La Bijude started even though the infantry were not ready until 10.00. By that time the situation was obscure due to poor light but the Crocodiles were reported to be very effective, the flails do not seem to have been used. Only half the position was captured before dusk, and that was abandoned. All tanks were withdrawn at 10.30pm and rallied to the rear close to the brigade HQ.

Next morning the site was reconnoitred by 'A' squadron and then a repeat of the previous evening's assault, but with a different battalion, commenced at 10.30am. It went in behind a creeping barrage moving at 100 yards each 13 minutes. The barrage was augmented by smoke fired by 'A' squadron from Epron and HE from a squadron of another regiment to the west. The infantry suffered some casualties from the artillery fire. The Hussars' adjutant thought, rather caustically, this was their fault for not being able to read the map properly. All efforts to halt the shoot failed. As a consequence of the casualties the infantry refused to follow the barrage and would not move until the shoot was complete, at midday. The tanks had reached the forward edge of the objective at 11.00am. There was little resistance, and a few prisoners were picked up.

That really completed the operation from the tanks' point of view. The regiment lost six tanks, had one officer wounded, one other rank killed and six wounded. It claimed to have knocked out six Panzer IVs.

Comments
This brief account has illustrated a case of infantry/tank cooperation not working well. There were several reasons for this.

Although the senior officers had two days to consider the operation there were no rehearsals and the tanks moved from the coast, where they had been enjoying a break, almost directly into their forming up place. In addition, the infantry and tanks had not worked together before, and it was the infantry's first time in action. One consequence of this general lack of experience was that they found it difficult to recover from the break down of communications, for example the use of runners is never mentioned even though the distances advanced were not great.

There was also a basic lack of sympathy between the tanks and infantry that only a long association would have thawed. The 13th/18th Royal Hussars (Queen Mary's Own) was a long established regular regiment. It has been on horses in India until late in 1938. It went to France in 1939 as mechanized divisional cavalry and was one of the last units to sail from Dunkirk, having actually done a little area cleaning on the beach. It had swum DD (amphibious) tanks ashore on 'D' day, and had been in action almost continuously since. During the La Bijude-Epron operation the CO was the Earl of Feversham. The infantry, on the other hand, were not regular, not experienced and not socially exclusive.

The Hussars did not help by insisting on maintaining their exclusive officers' mess, and upholding the highest standards in it. As one CO put it he did not like his officers living '*mucko chummo*' with their men!

It may be suspected that this regiment did not have a high regard for the infantry it was to support. Its adjutant referred to the Brigadier as '*Old Fryer*', and described the brigade as '*anything but impressive*'. No doubt all this would have been ironed out if the regiment and brigade had been associated for some weeks but this was not Field Marshall Montgomery's way. He viewed the armoured brigades as totally interchangeable units to be slotted in and out of armoured divisions and sent to support infantry divisions as required. No doubt this looked neat on maps and was efficient in planning terms, but could have its disadvantages on the ground.

Note: this account has been based on Squadron War Diaries made available by Home HQ, Light Dragoons.

The 6th Guards Tank Brigade at Caumont

The brigade arrived in Normandy on 20th July and was in action on the 30th, in Operation Bluecoat. This operation was mounted at short notice in response to a request by the Americans who were in the process of breaking out from St Lo. It involved three infantry divisions and an armoured division in the initial assault, and had a further armoured division in reserve. The main objective of the operation was the Bois du Homme ridge. The 43rd Division was to make the central thrust and capture the eastern end of the ridge, Hill 361. The 15th (Scottish) Division was to cover the 43rd Division's right flank and capture the western end of the ridge, Hill 309. The tank brigade was to support this division.

The brigade's order of battle was:
Commander Brigadier GL Verney
    HQ 6th Guards Tank Brigade

70

4th Tank Battalion, Grenadier Guards
4th Tank Battalion, Coldstream Guards
3rd Tank Battalion, Scots Guards
under command:

Lothian and Border Yeomanry, one squadron (Sherman Crabs)

141st Regiment RAC, The Buffs, one squadron (Crocodiles)

Each tank Battalion had 58 tanks, 18 in each of three squadrons, four in RHQ. The tanks were armed with a mix of two 75-mm guns for one 6-pdr.

The brigade received orders in the evening of 28th July and was on the move within two hours. It made a very difficult night march, 14 miles as the crow flies but much further by country lanes, and was in position to the north of Caumont, which is on high ground, next morning. It had only that day to liaise with the 15th (Scottish) Division, carry out reconnaissance and generally get ready.

Facing the attacking force was the German advanced position based on Lutaine Wood and the village of Sept Vents. Then, five miles further south was the objective, Hill 309, the number being the height in metres above sea level. The countryside was the usual bocage, close country with small fields bounded by thick hedges growing on thick earthen banks, and orchards. The obvious route to follow was the main Caumont-Vire road, running almost due south. *(See Sketch 3)*

Between the German advanced position and the objective was the German main line of resistance which ran through Le Homme, Hill 226, Les Loges and La Morichesse les Mares. Between these positions, which were over two miles apart, there was very little, a few MG crews and riflemen. German riflemen were usually called 'snipers'.

The German defence was becoming stretched. The bulk of the armour, which included the best troops, was further to the east fighting against British attempts to break through in the Caen area, all other available troops were being redeployed against the Americans. The assault from Caumont, therefore, came as a surprise.

The basic plan was that the Grenadiers tanks would support an infantry attack on Sept Vents and Lutaine Wood in the morning, this had to be done to a strict timetable so that full advantage could be taken of a creeping barrage to be fired when the other two tank battalions were to escort an infantry battalion to Hervieux and Les Loges. Once these locations were occupied the Grenadiers would escort troops from a different brigade on to Hill 309. It was an ambitious plan.

The attack went in at 8.0 next morning, 30th July, Two squadrons of tanks supported two companies attacking Sept Vents, and one supported one company at Lutaine Wood. They followed a short artillery barrage which created so much dust and smoke that visibility was greatly reduced.

Sept Vents fell easily. The tanks attempted to follow the infantry in the approved manner, but this was not Salisbury Plain and the difficulty of bocage meant that the tanks could not go where the infantry could, so the tanks found themselves advancing regardless of which infantry unit they were with. The approach to the village was funnelled through a sunken lane, an obvious fact that the defenders took advantage of, and five tanks were knocked out on mines. Some Crabs were called in to flail the route which they did even though they lost two Crabs on mines. Though the infantry easily cleared the village it must be noted that, because of mines and long range small arms (SA) and mortar fire, it was not till 3.0 pm that it was safe for wheeled vehicles to pass through.

Lutaine Wood was as easily taken, but by different means. Two of the Grenadiers officers were killed by SA fire and, as the tanks could not function well in a wood some Crocodiles were called in to burn it. One Churchill got behind the wood and cruised around shooting at any Germans it could find. The attacking infantry seem to have done little more than collect prisoners and occupy the remains of the wood. By 8.30am the German advanced position in front of 15th Division had been captured.

There was then a short lull before the next phase. A creeping barrage was to start at 9.30 to precede the troops as far as the intermediate objectives of Hervieux and Les Loges. The start line was 1,000 yards south of Sept Vents and Lutaine Wood, but unfortunately because of the difficult country, and mortar and SA fire, particularly between the two strongpoints, the infantry for phase two could not get there in time. Seeing this, and not wanting to lose the benefit of the barrage, the brigadier instructed the tanks to advance without their infantry. So, at 9.30 the tanks of the Coldstream Guards advanced to the east of the main road and, to their left, the Scots Guards advanced south towards Les Loges, leaving one squadron with the infantry.

This squadron advanced but slowly. Each hedge was one bound. The infantry, 2nd Argyll and Sutherland Highlanders, would peer through the hedge to ensure that there were no German AFVs in view, then the tanks would burst through the hedge and advance into the middle of the field, halt and shoot up the next hedge and anywhere else where Germans might be. Then the infantry would sprint to the next hedge and the process start again. This, naturally, was a tactic that would not work in the face of dug-in AT guns, but the advanced echelon of tanks had obviated that threat.

The Coldstreamers, advancing with two squadrons forward, were at Hervieux at 12.00 midday having met no opposition except SA fire. The Scots Guards halted at 12.15, at some distance short of Les Loges, hoping that the infantry would catch up, but they were disappointed in this, so after an hour they continued on. Their right squadron could not pass through Les Loges without infantry so it veered left and joined the other forward squadron on Hill 226 where it soon started to feel a little vulnerable.

The second phase was complete by 3.0 pm, and phase three required the Coldstream Guards to move from Hervieux to Hill 309. This objective was bombed by Marauder medium bombers at 4.0 and the guardsmen had to withdraw a short distance to give the bombers the prescribed safety margin. Unfortunately very few of the infantry battalion, the Glasgow Highlanders, which the guards should have supported in its assault on Hill 309, had arrived. Even worse, 43rd Division, on the left which should have been thrusting towards the Bois du Homme was making very disappointing progress. It was up to the commander of 15th Division, General MacMillan, and Brigadier Verney to decide if the advance should be called off or if it should continue. If it were to continue it must do so immediately to take advantage of the bombing.

The order was given for the Coldstream Guards to go. The small number of the Glasgow Highlanders that had got forward rode on the tanks, the remainder were urged forward to catch the tanks up and were to be escorted forward from Sept Vents by the Grenadiers.

The Coldstream tanks moved south by the main road but the leading squadron came across some German opposition at La Morichesse les Mares, and the Colonel decided to change direction and veer east directly towards Hill 309. The ground was a little boggy but the excellent cross-country mobility of the Churchills pulled them through and, at 7.0 pm the bulk of the battalion was on the summit of Hill 309. Perhaps the defenders had not recovered from the effects of the bombing.

Not quite all the tanks made it. One troop bogged down and one of its tanks tipped on its side. This caused a grenade in the turret to detonate, badly injuring three of the crew. The troop leader was captured by some Germans escorting a self-propelled AT gun. A tank was knocked out by an AT shot which killed the turret crew. It was said to come from a Panther but was just as likely to be from an AT gun. The tank had been the spare rear-link and had been travelling well to the rear of the fighting squadrons. On reaching La Morichesse it continued southward in error, straight into the enemy's line of fire.

The situation at 7.0 pm was that the objective had been reached, but now there would be something of a race to see if infantry reinforcements could be moved up before the Germans could mount a counter-attack.

The Grenadier tanks, carrying infantry, moved off from Sept Vents as soon as possible, but were held up at Hervieux for a considerable time by a traffic jam with the division's carriers. When they reached La Morichesse the leading tank was knocked out by an AT gun, presumably the same gun that hit the Coldstream tank, so, as the Colonel of the Coldstream Guards was demanding reinforcements urgently, the infantry dismounted and struck out following the Coldstream's cross-country route. However they made but slow progress as there were plenty of German riflemen and MG crews around, who had not fired on the Coldstream tanks, but now opened up on the infantry.

The Grenadier tanks, being stuck between La Morichesse and Hervieux were ordered to return north. This got them in another jam with the carriers. They were then ordered to leave the road and proceed towards Hill 309, which they did, and they passed the night some way to the north of the hill. Next day they commenced a series of small actions aimed at La Ferriere au Doyen.

The majority of the infantry arrived around dusk, at 8.30 pm, but small parties were coming in all through the night. The infantry's AT guns were man-handled forward as the carriers towing them could not cross the soft ground. The Coldstream tanks pulled back around 300 yards from the crest as the infantry set up their perimeter.

The next day started worryingly when one tank on the left was hit by an AT round from La Ferriere au Doyen, but the Germans on the whole were quiet. The 11th Armoured Division was coming up on the right and had reached La Martin du Besaces, which no doubt was enough for the Germans to cope with. The tanks were replenished with fuel and ammunition. This was brought up in three-ton vehicles to La Morishesse and then had to be loaded onto half-tracks because of the soft going.

The counter-attack came the next day, 1st August. The tanks came under heavy fire from self-propelled AT guns. But there were no hits. The German vehicles seem to have been rather unadventurous, and even though the new 6-pdr APDS rounds were bouncing off them, they stayed at long range.

The Scots Guards on Hill 226 had a more unfortunate time. Their infantry battalion arrived, with the third tank squadron, at about 4.0 pm on 30th July, but as they were without their AT guns the tanks had to stay with them to defend the infantry against any armoured counter-attacks. The tanks stayed forward and the infantry took up a position some way behind the tanks. This was hard to understand since a major threat to the tanks would have been tank hunting parties creeping forward and infantry should have been posted to prevent this. However before night fell it was shown that the threat was from self-propelled AT guns, not panzerfausts.

At 6.0 pm the tanks were hit by concentrated mortar fire, which killed one officer, then AT fire came from a wood 300 yards to the left rear. Had the infantry kept up with the tanks as planned this wood would have been checked, but as the plan assumed that it would have been cleared by the 43rd Division, it was ignored. The first three rounds coming from the wood knocked out a whole troop on the east flank. Then two self-propelled AT guns, covered by a third, burst out of the wood and charged through the Scots Guards tanks, knocking out a further eight. They disappeared down the front slope of the hill. As they left they were engaged by the surviving tanks and it may be that the suspension of one was damaged. These AFVs were identified as Jagdpanthers and this was one of the first occasions when they had been seen, they mounted 88-mm guns and may well have been more effective standing off and engaging the Churchills at long range, presenting as targets only their impenetrable glacis plates. After this shock the Scots Guards were left in peace on Hill 226.

The failure of the German counter-attacks marked the end of this part of the operation for the 6th Guards Tank Brigade.

Comments

This chapter has shown how the use of Infantry Tanks varied throughout the Second World War. At the start of the war the Matilda I and II tanks were all but invulnerable to the AT guns of the day, consequently a squadron of Matildas could drive almost wherever it wanted to. This was reflected in manuals of the day that put an echelon of tanks in front of the attacking infantry. This was the situation in the Arras counter-attack and Operation Compass, but it was to change as soon as the Germans had developed AT guns that were effective against the Matilda's thick armour. This change was demonstrated in

Operation Battleaxe, from then on the deployment of Infantry Tanks was more circumspect.

Operation Battleaxe also showed how effective AT minefields could be, and steps were taken to produce vehicles that would overcome the problem. This was the start of the development of specialised armour which, finally, would to a large degree, replace Infantry tanks in the assault of prepared defences.

The great disadvantage which early Infantry tanks laboured under was their main armament which was the 2-pdr. As this gun fired only solid shot the tanks could only engage AT guns with their MGs. As the German AT guns had shields it is not surprising that sometimes tanks actually ran over AT guns, not being able to get at them any other way. Modern manuals insist that tanks are capable of 'shock action', but in reality it is very much an act of desperation.

Throughout the war the tanks were steadily up-gunned, but right up to the end the main armament of Infantry tanks was not quite up to the required standard. However the issue of the 75-mm firing a reasonable HE shell did allow the tanks to seriously engage AT guns.

The examples given of British tanks supporting infantry in the bocage have illustrated the immense difficulty they experienced. There is no doubt that the new procedures introduced by Montgomery had a bad effect, but even so whatever manuals prescribed was just not going to work in the bocage. There was, though, a general trend for the tanks to follow the infantry when encountering heavy resistance; but as German resistance crumbled, for the tanks to take the lead. The secret of success was for the infantry and armoured units to have trained together and to have had time to work out standard drills and procedures. The 6th Guards Tank Brigade was generally successful at Caumont, at least partly because it had trained for many months with the 15th (Scottish) Division in England. Conversely the 13th/18th Royal Hussars hardly knew the 59th Division and seem to have had a contempt for it.

If the answer lay in the infantry and tanks training together it may be wondered if armoured brigades should not have been permanently associated with particular infantry divisions. This is a tempting concept, there having been a similar number of tank and armoured brigades in Normandy as there were infantry divisions. There were eight British and Canadian tank and armoured brigades, though one was disbanded during the campaign, and eleven infantry divisions, including one disbanded during the campaign, and one airborne division. However the lack of flexibility resulting from such an organisation would have more than counter balanced any advantage. For example the 31st Armoured Brigade, and others, being issued with steadily increasing quantities of specialised armour, periodically came under the command of 79th Armoured Division. There can be little doubt that the organisation settled on was the best available at the time.

There was an attempt made in 1942 in six infantry divisions to improve infantry-tank cooperation by replacing a brigade in each by an armoured brigade. This organisation was given a fair trial but it was concluded that it resulted in a too great reduction in infantry strength, and it was discontinued in 1943. It is interesting to note that the Soviet Union settled on a similar concept for its infantry divisions.

The major problem was lack of communication between tanks and infantry, resulting in them becoming separated. Once the tank commander had closed down he was really *incommunicado*. Radios were neither plentiful nor robust enough to meet the need, and the Germans deliberately targeted the operators. The infantry/tank telephone was but seldom used in action. So there was no real alternative to a lengthy discussion between tank and infantry commanders before each tactical move. Once the move started the bocage forced the two arms apart. Soldiers could worm their way through thick undergrowth and hedges, but most of these beat Shermans and some of them beat Churchills, so the tanks had to find a way round.

There was, however, a way round this problem. The Americans produced the 'rhino', sometimes called the 'hedge chopper', or the 'Cullin hedgerow device' after the inventor, or the 'Sherman prong'. It was essentially five or six approximately foot-long spikes welded to the lower front of the tank. The principle was that these spikes dug into the base of the bocage bank preventing the tank being deflected upwards so allowing it to drive a passage through the hedge. It was first demonstrated, in strict secrecy, on 22nd July, and after that the Americans fitted as many as possible before the end of the bocage fighting. It was really an obvious device and dramatically increased the mobility of the tanks and the effectiveness of tank-infantry cooperation. Unfortunately it seems that no Churchills were modified with this device, but some British Shermans were, particularly in 4th Armoured Brigade which operated for some time next to the Americans.

In the most difficult going that tanks were deployed in, Churchills showed themselves to be more tactically mobile than either Shermans or Cromwells, and it is surprising to note that in operational moves Churchill units kept up with armoured divisions driving the faster tanks. Churchills of the 6th Guards Tank Brigade supporting the 6th Airborne Division covered 240 miles in 12 days in the pursuit to the Weser, keeping up with the 7th and 11th Armoured Divisions. Even in a purely non-tactical administrative move on tracks, from Flers to the Seine, in September after the Normandy campaign, the Guards Tank Brigade kept up with the Guards Armoured Division with a negligible number of mechanical break-downs.

By the time of the Normandy campaign British Cruiser Tanks were being eclipsed by Shermans. It is true that one British armoured division, out of three, was equipped mostly with Cromwells, and later partly with Comets, but perhaps if the Shermans were available production capacity would have been better deployed on the development of what was to be called the 'Main Battle Tank'.

In view of the Churchill's greater mobility when compared to the Sherman, and also its greater survivability based on its thicker armour and smaller tendency to burst into flames when hit, it may be wondered if this production should have been concentrated on Churchills. Unfortunately there was one aspect of the Churchill design that was inferior to that of the Sherman, that was, typical of British tanks, the narrow turret ring. As a result of this the Churchill, unlike the Sherman, could not be up-gunned to mount the 17-pdr. This was compensated for tactically by backing Churchills up with M10 Tank Destroyers, but in terms of design the Churchill was at a dead end. A batch of six 'Super Churchills', or 'Black Princes', was built, making space for the bigger gun by widening and lengthening the hull, but the extra weight resulting from this slowed the tank down to only 11 mph, and the army preferred the Centurion.

Chapter 6: Specialised Armour

The driving force for the development of Specialised Armour was the increasing difficulty of attacking prepared defences. This difficulty was shown in North Africa by the growing importance of mine warfare, and in Great Britain by the anticipated problems in overcoming the Atlantic Wall.

To solve these problems a series of vehicles was developed. There was a wide variety of these vehicles, the most important being:

> Crab flail tanks,
> AVREs,
> Bridging tanks,
> Flamethrowers.

Crab Flail Tanks

The Crab was the standard British mine clearing AFV of the war. Even though mine warfare was one of the great tactical innovations of the Second World War, the Great War had given an indication of what was to come and experiments had been carried out with rollers and ploughs attached to tanks. These had not been a great success and had not been followed up between the wars, but in the next war they were revived, only to meet with similar lack of success though one design, the Bullshorn, was used in the Normandy landings. The real success was the flail.

The Flail was first used at Alamein. It consisted of a steel drum mounted across the front of a tank and fitted with some heavy chains. The drum was rotated and the chains flailed the ground exploding any mines ahead of the tank. The early versions were powered by auxiliary motors, and were fitted on a variety of tanks, Matildas, Valentines and Grants. When they were tried on Shermans it was found that the auxiliary motor caused problems and the flail was most conveniently, and reliably, powered via the tank's power pack. Such a tank was designated the 'Crab', but it is common to see the words 'Crab' and 'Flail' used interchangeably.

As is obvious the flail could easily miss mines in rough ground though this problem was largely corrected in the Crab II in which the rotating drum was mounted on arms that automatically kept the drum at the same height. The great disadvantage with the flail system was that it raised clouds of dust, so highly visible station keeping lights were mounted on the rear of the Crabs and a lane marking system was introduced which fired pickets into the ground.

AVREs

The Armoured Vehicle Royal Engineers was the standard RE assault vehicle of the second half of the war. It was essentially a Churchill tank emptied of pretty-well everything, that included turret basket, co-driver and seat, ammunition bins and main armament. The space made available was occupied by engineering stores and sappers. This process was tried with a Sherman and a Ram, the Canadian tank, but it worked best with the Churchill partly because of the convenient access through the pannier door in the side of the hull.

The main armament, originally the 2-pdr then the 6-pdr, was replaced by a large calibre, 290-mm, spigot mortar. This mortar was designed by Colonel Blacker who also designed the Blacker Bombard and the PIAT. It had already been mounted and tested on other tanks so its characteristics were well known. It delivered a very formidable 40-lb projectile, often called a 'Flying Dustbin', but only up to a range of 80 yards. The range of the mortar was so short that sights were hardly necessary, and the first AVREs landed at Normandy did not have any. Specially designed telescopic sights became available in August 1944.

Because the mortar was muzzle-loading, the loading procedure was complex. There was no longer a co-driver, so a hole was cut in the armour above his seat position, this hole had a sliding cover. The gunner would traverse the turret so that the mortar's muzzle was just above this hole. The loader then fed in the next round via a loading trough. A good crew could go through this process in 20 seconds, but no doubt enemy MG fire would slow this down.

The AVRE's greatest contribution to the war was in the varieties of special devices that could be mounted on it, some of them will be mentioned later, the most important one in the next paragraph. In its basic form, what was termed 'General Purpose', GP, configuration it carried 26 mortar rounds, some Bangalore Torpedoes and hand demolition charges, among other RE stores.

Bridging tanks

The Small Box Girder, SBG, bridge was 34 feet long, weighed four tons and could carry 40 tons. It was carried on the front of an ARVE, hoisted up near vertically like a drawbridge, this made the tank nose heavy and difficult to control. It was sometimes called an 'assault bridge'.

The Churchill bridgelayer was a similar bridge, but capable of bearing 60 tons. It was carried horizontally on a turretless Churchill and was laid in position by hydraulic equipment operated by the driver. This version was often called a 'scissors bridge'.

There was a variation on this theme called the 'Ark'. This was a turretless Churchill with a ramp at both ends. The tank would be driven into a gap and the ramps lowered then other vehicles could drive over it. The name of this vehicle seems to have been derived from the similarity of its flat top surface to that of an aircraft carrier, and the Ark Royal being the most well known aircraft carrier of the day.

Flamethrowers

The Crocodile was a simple modification to a standard Churchill. It involved a two-wheeled trailer, which was lightly armoured and weighed six and a half tons. It carried 400 gallons of fuel and five nitrogen bottles. The fuel was forced through a hose that ran through the length of the tank's hull and the flame projector replaced the hull MG. The hull gunner operated the flame projector. The flame thrower had a range of 80 to 120 yards and a trailer's worth of fuel would give 80 one second bursts.

The link between the trailer and the tank could be vulnerable to artillery, but in the case of damage, or if all the fuel was spent, the trailer could be jettisoned and the tank continue as a normal gun tank.

In North-West Europe all the vehicles listed here were controlled by the 79th Division. This list should also include the Kangaroo armoured personnel carriers, two regiments of which became incorporated in the division. Unfortunately the division regarded them as primarily an infantry and RASC concern, and seems to have taken little interest in their tactical possibilities. They will be considered as a separate class of vehicle, in Chapter 8.

Also within the 79th Division there was a wide range of amphibious vehicles that were used in the Walcheren operation and the Rhine crossing among other operations. These vehicles, though important, do not come under the infantry support classification and will not be considered here.

Canal Defence Lights

These vehicles (CDLs) have been included in this list for the sake of completeness. This is so because the CDL was a failure and not used in action. The CDL was essentially a searchlight mounted on a Grant Medium tank but with a device to make it flicker. It was developed as a private venture and demonstrated to the War Office in 1937. The

War Office was impressed, ordered the development to continue, and gave it its title to disguise its true nature.

In a totally separate development, in 1938, a trial was run by 1RTR, mounting spotlights on their tanks to improve night shooting. Improve it they did, but the Colonel noted that the lights should not be lit for more than fifteen seconds as that would make the tanks too easy targets. These lights were occasionally used in the early days in the desert, but their use soon faded away, there being little demand for continuous white light on the battlefield.

The CDL concept depended on the flicker which, it was believed, would entirely baffle enemy gunners. The plan was that an extended line of CDLs would advance, naturally at night, and their beams would create a series of inverted 'Vs' between and in front of them of total darkness, where the infantry could advance unseen.

The CDL development was highly sophisticated and carried out under maximum security, and perhaps it was this security which resulted in the concept not being thoroughly tried out during exercises. It is difficult to believe that the CDL tanks could survive at night, and the black 'Vs' would have told the German artillery and mortars exactly where the attacking infantry were. However that may be a three regiment brigade of CDL tanks was sent to France but never used except, later on, to provide ordinary spotlight illumination for the Rhine crossing.

Night operations were not much undertaken by the British in Normandy, but, as will be seen, Operation Totalise was carried out at night and it would be thought that there should have been a role for CDLs in it. Perhaps with all the security no-one knew that the CDLs were there. The ignoring of the CDLs was really the equivalent of having three armoured regiments put out of action, and represents a sad and avoidable waste of resources.

Specialised Armour Tactics

The tactics to be adopted by the four types of AFV listed in the previous section were dependent upon the task in hand and their characteristics. Consequently these tactics were simple. In all cases it was essential to beat down the defender's AT gunfire before the operation started. Specialised armour moved slowly and would be highly vulnerable. For best results they needed to be escorted by gun tanks which would respond quickly to unforeseen resistance.

If the task were breaching a minefield the flailing Crabs would advance into the minefield echeloned backwards to one side, tanks not flailing could provide fire support. When a flail detonated an AT mine at least one chain was blown off. A Crab could account for 12 to 14 mines before its flail was useless. When flailing a Crab could only progress at one and a quarter miles per hour and it raised clouds of dust so maintaining correct alignment was not easy. At night tracer ammunition could be fired over the Crabs to assist in this. One Crab could flail a path nine and a half feet wide. The standard gap was 24 feet wide, and to achieve this three Crabs were required. Crabs usually flailed 'echelon right', that is the second and third Crabs driving a little behind the Crab to their left. Echelon right was the usual formation because the driver sat on the left and would only be able to see and keep station with a tank on that side. Usually a troop of five tanks would be allocated to one gap, three flailing, two in reserve.

Major difficulties could occur if a Crab struck a mine, this would usually result in a broken track. The area round the Crab would have to be swept by hand, slowing the process down.

When the Crab was flailing its turret had to be traversed rear, but when not it could function as an ordinary gun tank. For long distance travel the flail drum was wrapped in canvas to keep the chains out of the way.

If the task were general demolition the AVRE would take its load of sappers and stores as close to the obstacle as possible and, if it could get within range and the target was an appropriate one, it would engage it with its mortar. As the campaign progressed so various devices were mounted on the front of AVREs. The AVRE, then, had to get close enough to its target for these devices, which were usually for placing explosive charges, to do their job. Explosive charges and Bangalore torpedoes could be fired from inside the AVRE but usually had to be set up by sappers on their feet. This would be a hazardous task if absolute fire supremacy had not been achieved.

One of the AVREs devices could be a SBG bridge and the above comments apply to its use. The SBG bridge, being so high, was highly visible and its position would make it plain to the enemy where the breach was intended. The scissors bridge was rather better in this respect. For best results both would be guided into position by a man of foot. In places in Italy where rivers were cut very deep the Ark could be very useful. In extreme cases one Ark could be driven in on top of another. For wide rivers Arks could be driven one across another until a causeway was created. In this context it is interesting to note that the Russians crossed the Donets in August 1943 on a causeway of a double row of T34s, presumably with their turrets removed, driving one over the other into the river. The resulting causeway being a few inches under water.

The tactics for the flamethrower were the most basic of all. The target was identified then the Crocodiles would drive up to about eighty yards of it and hose it down. They were very effective weapons and much feared by the Germans.

As can be seen few man-made obstacles could stand long against an attack by specialised armour. In particular pillboxes, which had been almost invulnerable in the Great War, were not a great challenge. They were systematically taken out by following the 'drill' which was steadily refined after Normandy. Firstly the target pillbox would be isolated, either by smoke or by destroying any source of supporting fire. Secondly flails would clear a path up to it. Then an AVRE would hit it with a 'flying dustbin'. Finally, if required, a flame-thrower would hose it down. The petard would usually have cracked open the embrasure to let the flame in. This last stage was not always necessary.

An alternative ending would be 'letter posting'. A tank would drive up to around ten yards of the embrasure, and its gun would be sighted by the loader looking through the barrel. The sights could not be used as they were displaced too far from the barrel. The shell fired in this manner would be fatal to the pillbox. Interestingly modern tank gunners cannot use their optical sights at ranges of less than 200 yards as the sights develop the condition of parallax.

No tactical manual was produced for Specialised Armour during the war, but soon after the war ended the manual 'The Characteristics and Employment of Specialised Armour'(see note) was written. This manual was not published and only a few 'Roneo' copies were produced. It is reasonable to assume that the principles and procedures covered in it were in force at the time of the assault of Blerick, on 3rd December 1944, and sections of it will be quoted along with a brief description of that operation.

Note:
This manual has been reprinted by Military Library Research Service Ltd

Chapter 7: Specialised Armour in Action

Although there had been an appreciation of the necessity for specialised armour almost since the first use of tanks their evolution really began as the preferred method of breaching the minefields at Alamein. The need for a wider range of specialised AFVs was not appreciated until the battle on the Mareth Line, but from then on development proceeded apace.

The driving force of this development was the anticipated difficulty of making a landing in Europe. The Dieppe raid had shown that Infantry Tanks by themselves could be massacred, so a wide range of Specialised Armour was assembled to support the British and Canadian landings. However it seems that there was initially little realisation of how useful these vehicles would be for the fighting inland, probably because of an exaggerated belief in the war-winning potential of divisions of Cruiser Tanks, and the demand for them seems to have come as a bit of a surprise.

After Normandy specialised armour saw extensive service with most major formations right up to the end of the war, but remarkably little service with armoured divisions. It could, just, be that if the Guards Armoured Division had had a few bridging tanks with it for the drive to Arnhem then Operation Market-Garden might have been a success.

The use of specialised armour will be illustrated by considering the two actions mentioned in North Africa, followed by the Normandy Landings, and then the assaults on two prepared positions, assaults that would have cost the attackers hundreds of casualties had specialised armour been missing.

Flails at Alamein

At Alamein in October 1942 the 8th Army faced two main problems, the Axis minefields and the AT guns behind them. Breaching these minefields was to be the first use of what was to become termed 'Specialised Armour'.

The threat of AT mines had been taken seriously for some time, particularly since the assault of Sidi Omar, on 21st November 1941, one of the first actions of 13th Corps in Operation Crusader. In this action two infantry battalions of 7th Indian Brigade supported by the Matildas of 42 and 44 RTR assaulted the Italian-manned strongpoint on the Egypt-Libyan border. The strongpoint had an extensive minefield to its south and east, the anticipated direction of attack. When 13th Corps troops had taken up position to the west and north of the strongpoint mines were moved those sides which were obviously now the sides that would be attacked. Patrols did not detect the new minefield.

The strongpoint was taken by assault, but at a cost of 500 infantry casualties and 35 Matildas knocked out. The vehicle casualties were caused mostly by mines, and the infantry casualties by the sudden lack of tank support.

It was plain that something had to be done about this threat so, in 1942, the 8th Army set up the School of Minefield Clearance in Egypt, and, as the principle of the flail had been accepted, the School had some Matilda Scorpions made from Matildas that were being withdrawn from front line service and so were available for conversion. This involved a Ford V8 engine, self-contained with its drive train and cooling system, being mounted on the right hand side (from the driver's point of view) of the tank. The engine and its operator were encased in a lightly armoured box. This engine drove the rotating drum which was set well in front of the tank on girders. This variant was the

Scorpion I and twenty-four were ready in time for Alamein, which was not many in view of the scope of the battle. Apart from the 7th Armoured Division the units they were issued to tended to keep them back for emergencies

The bulk of the fighting on the first day of the battle was done by 30th Corps in the northern part of the front, but the most impressive use of Scorpions was made by the 7th Armoured Division, which was to make a diversionary attack in the south. Here the Axis defence was based on two minefields, codenamed JANUARY and FEBRUARY. Each of these was around 1,000 yards deep and they were around 4,000 yards apart. The plan was to breach both minefields in the first night.

Most divisions involved in the initial phase of the battle created a Minefield Task Force. Each division's task force was unique, but the point of them all was to have the units involved in breaching the minefields under one commander. In this case the task force was based on the 44th Reconnaissance Regiment.

This regiment was the reconnaissance regiment of the 44th Division that was manning the front line. The 7th Armoured Division was to pass through this division on its way to JANUARY. The regiment had originally been issued in England with motorcycles, Humber light reconnaissance cars, Bren gun carriers and lorries. This was sensible for operations in Europe but not for the desert. The motorcycles and light reconnaissance cars were no use on sand and were sent to the rear. Then the regiment went through a series of changes until in early September it was the basis of the Minefield Task Force under the command of 22nd Armoured Brigade, which itself had only just become a permanent part of the 7th Armoured Division. For the impending action the number of carriers was tripled to a total of 38 by taking carriers from the rest of the division. They were organised in two squadrons.

The Minefield Task Force comprised of two separate groups, the breaching force and the bridgehead group. The breaching force was 44th Reconnaissance Regiment, six Scorpions and an RE field squadron. The bridgehead group consisted of the Royal Scots Greys, on Shermans, four companies of the KRRC and an AT battery.

The task force trained hard for the operation. They were to drive four lanes through both minefields. The lanes were numbered 1 to 4 from north to south. Numbers 1 and 2, and 3 and 4, were 50 yards apart, but there was a 500 yard gap between the two pairs of lanes. The plan was to lead with one Scorpion per lane, with two in reserve. Once through JANUARY the carrier squadrons were to fan out, spread panic among the defenders, and protect the RE from small arms fire, then the Scorpions and RE were to proceed to FEBRUARY.

The breaching force was to be followed by the bridgehead group. This was based on the Scots Greys whose Sherman tanks would follow along the two inside lanes, also a company of the KRRC would drive along each of the lanes. The tanks would be followed by the AT battery. The task of the bridgehead group was, as the name implies, to dig in and defend the exits from JANUARY against any possible counter-attack.

The Minefield Task Force was to be followed by the tanks of 22nd Armoured Brigade. It can be seen that the plan was an ambitious one. The Corps Commander, General Horrocks, placed great faith in the Scorpions, which may be the reason that the plans were wildly optimistic.

Gapping should have started at 9.40pm 23rd October 1942, but the task force arrived at the start line 10 minutes late, even so number 2 lane was through by 1.40am. The Scorpion was damaged by a mine and hit by an AT gun shortly before clearing the gap and the job was finished by sappers by hand. Number 1 lane was through at 4.30, but the exit was just in front of an Axis position, so it was hard to take advantage of.

The southern two lanes caused greater difficulty for two reasons, firstly because the defenders had laid a small number of mines in front of the forward edge of the minefield. This caused the task force to deploy and the Scorpions to start flailing too soon. Secondly the going was very soft. The Scorpions tended to overheat but were kept running by the efforts of their crews. Lane 3 was through at 2.15 but the Scorpion was disabled, presumably by a mine, at the lane's exit. Lane 4 was cleared by hand by 12.30, the Scorpion having been knocked out by artillery about three quarters of the way through. The gun that was responsible was located, by its muzzle flashes, at a range of 2,000 yards. A Vickers MMG which was aboard a truck following close behind the Scorpion was brought into action and quickly wiped out the crew.

Casualties among the breaching force had been heavy and its commander informed the brigade commander that he could only drive two lanes through FEBRUARY. Gapping was timed to begin at 5.30am, but one gapping party could not get there in time and the other, as dawn started to break and enemy fire increased, could make no progress. The Brigade commander decided to call the operation off for the day and ordered the tanks back through JANUARY. Two of the KRRC companies dug in to defend the bridgeheads, the other two attacked and rounded up enemy personnel between the minefields.

The bulk of the task force stayed between the minefields during the day. Unfortunately some high ground, Himeimat, away five miles to the south, was in Axis hands. It had previously been captured by the Free (Fighting) French but a determined armoured counter-attack had retaken it. The problem for the French was that because of the soft sand they could not move their AT guns forward, so had nothing to fight the panzers with. Recapturing Himeimat gave the defenders good artillery observation making life very difficult for the brigade.

The attack was continued next night, but without Scorpions, none of which was fit for action, but with the assistance of an infantry brigade transferred to the division for this purpose. Two lanes were cleared by hand but tanks could not get through in face of the defender's fire. So in order to keep 7th Armoured Division in condition to be ready to move north the operation was called off.

The Corps commander was disappointed. Some days later he commented to the brigade commander, Brigadier Roberts, that he could have got through, but it is difficult to see how this could have been done without heavy casualties.

The Scorpions had shown themselves to be unreliable and prone to overheating, but were generally agreed to have done a good job. However it must be recorded that Roberts considered Horrocks' plan of breaching the minefields with '*Scorpions and masses of carriers*' to have been a '*ridiculous idea*'. Indeed when 44th Reconnaissance Regiment was withdrawn only four of its 38 carriers had survived, and it had lost over 113 personnel.

Failure at Mareth

Following their defeat at Alamein the Axis forces pulled right back to Tunisia, fighting several small scale delaying actions *en route*. The fact that the German troops, and large numbers of Italians, reached Tunisia in fighting condition was an indication that the RAF was still failing in its role of interdiction. This was a role that the RAF itself had proclaimed to be more important than close support.

The Axis command decided to defend the Mareth Line. This was a defensive system built by the French to keep the Italians out of that part of their empire. The Mareth line could hardly be called a 'Southern Maginot Line' as was done at the time, but the terrain could be used to produce a strong system. Observation posts were built on hills, batteries in concrete casemates, heavy guns in centres of resistance, barbed wire entanglements, trenches and fields of AT rails typical of French fortifications. The main feature was the Wadi Zigzaou, lengths of which had been scarped to produce a significant AT obstacle. Where this was not possible it was backed up by an AT ditch.

The centres of resistance were redoubts for one or two infantry companies, though some could accommodate a battalion, and consisted of groups of pillboxes. The battalion sized redoubts could be 1,200 yards wide and 400 yards deep. The pillboxes were arranged to be mutually supporting, some connected by tunnels. The trenches all had concrete revetments. Many of these French AT pillboxes could not accommodate the German 50-mm guns, and these had to be deployed in less satisfactory positions. The French believed that they had little to fear from heavy artillery which, they thought, could not be moved across the sand or survive in the open, but the fortifications were designed to survive air attack.

No doubt the line was as good as could be hoped for in view of the limited resources available, and no doubt it was not really expected to be attacked by a first class army. Its great disadvantage was that it could be outflanked to the south. The dramatic improvements in the cross country capability of vehicles had not been anticipated by its planners. Judged dispassionately it would have been better to have built the line more to the west either at the Tebaga Gap, 20 miles, or at the Gabes Gap, a further 15 miles to the west. Probably imperial hubris demanded that the frontier be defended. The defenders were three fresh Italian infantry divisions and a German motorised division, the 90th Light, presumably with only a few AFVs. There was a panzer division in reserve.

The Mareth Line had to be breached, the plan was to break into the line at the northern end and roll it up. The main position was based on the Wadi Zigzaou, and an outpost line was based on the Wadi Zeuss about three miles in front. It took a few days to build up supplies then the two pronged attack on the outpost line was launched in the moonlit night of 16th/17th March 1943.

The main, northern, attack met little resistance, and advanced a mile past the outpost line. A second attack a few miles to the south by two Guards battalions turned out to be a disaster. Their objective was some low bare hills, and the battalions followed a creeping barrage across the wadi onto the hills and right into a minefield. There were thousands of 'S' (anti-personnel) mines, these had been encountered before but never in such quantities. There were plenty of Teller (anti-tank) mines that blew up all the carriers coming with ammunition or trying to pick up the wounded, and the troops came under heavy mortar fire. Even though the objectives were finally reached, casualties had been so heavy, 363 and 159 for the two battalions, that they could not be held against enemy infiltration and the battalions were withdrawn.

This disaster showed how important a careful reconnaissance by patrols was. Even so there would be no delay in putting in the attack on the main Mareth position, and next day a further attack put a battalion in a position overlooking the crossing. The main attack was set for the night of 20th/21st March.

This attack was very well rehearsed, and the objective well reconnoitred. Patrols including tank commanders had crossed the Wadi Zigzaou and pronounced it not much of an AT obstacle. It was 80 yards wide with near vertical banks up to 20 feet high in places, so the infantry had to carry ladders to get in and out. The water in the wadi was very shallow, the bottom firm, probably an old ford, and mined. Engineers would make gaps in the bank and clear the mines. Set back roughly 100 yards from the wadi was an AT ditch, this was 10 feet deep, of 'V' cross-section, mined and wired. In front of it was a row of rails standing about two feet high, the brigade account mistakenly calls them 'dragons teeth'. They were not serious obstacles as they had not been cemented into place, had they been the plan would have been to cross them on fascines. The ditch was covered by two battalion-sized redoubts, supported by three-company sized redoubts, there were the usual infantry trenches behind it. Further back there was a system of military roads that would be important in bringing forward the counter-attacking units.

The AT ditch was to be blown in by the engineers and crossed with the use of fascines if these proved necessary. Each of the tanks carried one. They were ten feet long and of two different diameters: three feet for use in the ditch, two feet for use in the wadi. They were carried in front of the turret above the driver's position so the turret had to be traversed to three o'clock to accommodate one, and the gun could not be used. Experiments were carried out firing tracer at a fascine and it was found not to burn. Unfortunately the design of the Valentine did not help. The exhaust runs along the side of the hull to a point in front of the turret. Inevitable the fascine would come to rest on it and several fascines were set on fire due to this. The attacking infantry would have plenty of air support, artillery and fifty-one Valentine tanks in reserve. They had first to defeat a position known as the Bastion in front of the wadi, then cross a minefield, then the wadi and then the AT ditch

The assault on the Bastion went well. The attackers were the Green Howards, they had formed units of assault troops known as 'thugs', and after heavy fighting these assault troops won through. This success allowed the advance through the minefield. This was done with the aid of three Scorpions which did a good job and there were few casualties due to mines. The attack across the wadi was made by two battalions of the Durham Light Infantry 1,200 yards apart at sites marked as fords. The wadi was more of an obstacle than expected. A heavy downpour in the hills to the south had deepened the water in it to around knee-deep. This was no obstacle to the infantry but it had the effect of softening the bottom which would prove disastrous. Initially things went well, covered by a heavy barrage, the infantry crossed and the engineers set to work bringing the sides down to made a crossing for the tanks.

The first four tanks crossed the wadi, dropped their fascines in the AT ditch and crossed it. The fifth broke through the crust of the wadi's bottom and sank up to its turret. This blocked the crossing. The engineers set to work building up a causeway but no further tanks crossed that night. The others did not try to cross during daylight as casualties among the engineers would have been prohibitive.

In the meantime the infantry had left the wadi, crossed the AT ditch, and proceeded to attack the Mareth line defences which had been reinforced by a German battalion and some German artillery. They carried on with this all the next day. It was painfully slow and costly fighting, clearing pits, trenches and tunnels. They made progress but the strength of well planned fortifications demonstrated itself even if, as the Regimental History states 'French blockhouses...looked more formidable than in fact they were'. The Germans reacted vigorously moving up AT guns. Their favoured tactic was to open up with heavy machine gun fire and when the tanks were tempted out to silence the MGs they would be hit by the AT guns. When night came two new infantry battalions and the remaining tanks crossed the wadi. Unfortunately the tanks made the crossing unusable for wheeled vehicles and, had lighter vehicles towing 6-pdr guns gone first, things would have been different. This also meant that the artillery FOO could not get forward. The next day progress started to pick up as the Italian defenders' morale started to crumple under the pounding artillery fire and large numbers surrendered. This weight of artillery fire, though, was not heavy enough to destroy the redoubts.

The engineers in the wadi had worked miracles particularly as the weather had produced a sharp shower that further deepened the water in the wadi considerably and, by midday on 22nd, they had made a route crossable by wheeled vehicles. Unfortunately they were just too late, at 12.30pm the German barrage came down, and at 1.40pm the counter attack started. The 15th Panzer Division, in reserve, had only thirty or so tanks but the 51 Valentines could not stand against them. All were armed with the 2-pdrs except for eight which had 6 pdrs. The tanks fought gallantly, putting down smoke and manœuvring in support of the infantry, but the odds were too great, and finally the Colonel was killed leading the RHQ troop in a desperate counter-attack. The real need of the infantry was towed 6-pdr guns, but they had none, and some tanks that went back across the wadi to bring some failed. The Valentines did not have hooks appropriate for towing guns, and attempts to lash the guns to the tanks failed as this prevented the tanks making the required sharp bends. The 6-pdr can be dismantled and carried in separate loads, it is not known why this was not done.

In the end the survivors were all forced back. It was not a rout, they fought doggedly all the way but the enemy was just too strong for them. Another brigade had been moved up but the attack was called off. The intensity of the fighting is shown by the casualties, out of the 900 DLI that went into the attack, two battalions in the first wave and one in the second, only 200 men came back. The last of a string of disasters for the DLI was one company being cut off during the retreat. The soldiers fixed bayonets and made a dash for it, but ran straight into a minefield.

The defeat could have been avoided if the 6-pdrs had been sent across the wadi directly after the first troop of tanks, but no doubt supporting the infantry in extending the bridgehead was given a higher priority. The 2-pdr Valentines were good enough for this task, probably better than the 6-pdr version. This was because some 6-pdr Valentines did not have a coaxial MG though the 6-pdr HE shells, if available, would have made up for this to some extent. Even so with prior planning and preparation it should have been possible to get the 6-pdr AT guns and FOO forward.

The artillery did not do well in this action. There were too few guns, roughly one every 100 yards, which was a third the density at Alamein, but still their failure to break up the counter-attack was depressing. Also air support should have been on hand, but the attacking units did not have good long range radios or an Air Liaison Officer forward with them. Finally it may be wondered if the years of desert fighting had resulted in engineering considerations not being accorded the necessary priority.

The attempt to penetrate the Mareth Line was a failure, and an unnecessary one. Plans were made to continue the assault at a different crossing point but as soon as Montgomery realised the situation he cancelled these and ordered the outflanking attack. The attack on the line could easily have been replaced by a demonstration. Montgomery took the view that the repulse fitted in with his master plan and the operation as a whole was a great success. He did admit to the loss of '*25 very old Valentines*'. Montgomery seems to have developed a strong disliking for infantry tanks which he was to display again in Normandy. He had actually been offered a brigade of Churchills for the Mareth battle, but turned them down. This was tragic. With their surprisingly good mobility, thick armour and 6-pdr guns, a few Churchills might just have swung the battle in favour of the British, and saved many casualties.

The tank vehicle casualties were a total of 33 Valentines, with 27 irreparable. The tank personnel casualties were eight dead, 30 wounded and four missing. That the personnel casualties were comparatively low is partly explained by the Valentine having a crew of only three, and partly by the engagements being at long range so crewmen abandoning crippled vehicles were not so likely to be shot down.

The Mareth battle made very clear the requirement for specialised armour. The extensive use of anti-personnel mines meant that breaching minefields by hand was a much more difficult task so flails would be more in demand. Also crossing the wadi would have been easy had there been some Arks available. Some ARVEs would have handled the fascines easily. Such points as these would have been noted by the 'D' day planners.

The Normandy Landings

The problem facing the invasion force was really similar to that facing any attempt to assault a prepared position, being how best to subdue enemy fire and assist the infantry forward across the beach and through the minefields and other obstacles into the enemy's defences.

The German policy was to stop the invaders on the beaches and to hit those troops that did get ashore with an immediate counter-attack. This policy was demanded by Rommel as a result of his appreciation of the way Allied air power would inhibit daytime movement, particularly on roads. This policy was not a very good one, but the best available, and doomed by the convoluted hierarchy not to work. This policy found expression in the construction of the 'Atlantic Wall', a system of beach defences, mostly in France.

There is no doubt that some of the remains of this system of defences are very impressive, but overall it was not. In fact the German commander in France, Von Rundstedt, regarded it as *'an enormous bluff'*, believing that the Allies could break through it almost at will. Rommel was in command of the Wall and he thought otherwise.

Initially the plan for the Wall was little more than the defence of the ports. The idea was that the Allies would have to capture a port to land their heavy weapons and other supplies. So if the ports could be denied them they would be easily overcome by the counter-attack and some fortifications were built to support this concept. The swing away from this system to one of defending all the beaches was required by Rommel's strategy.

The Wall, in theory, stretched 2,600 miles from within the Arctic Circle to the Spanish border, but it is only necessary to consider the length actually assaulted by the Allies. The

Wall's great strength lay in mines. Rommel, as a result of his North African experiences, was very interested in mines. Before he took charge, in January 1944, not a great deal had been done in this respect, but he had 6,500,000 mines laid. He was aiming at a total of 50,000,000. Some units, failing to keep up with Rommel's demands, put up dummy 'Achtung Minen' signs to hide that fact. In addition to mines there were extensive beach obstacles, many of which had mines or artillery shells attached. The defences on land, the 'Rommelbelt', were less formidable.

The Rommelbelt comprised strongpoints at roughly 1,000 yard intervals. These consisted of trenches, pillboxes and fortified buildings, and contained machine guns, one or two mortars and one or two field or AT guns. They were held by garrisons of from a platoon to a company in strength. The strongpoints were essential to the defensive scheme and were expected to put up a spirited resistance. This was spelt out in the Fuehrer Directive No 40 of 23rd March 1942 which stated that 'Fortified areas and strongpoints are to be held to the last. They must never be forced to surrender because of a shortage of ammunition, rations or water.' The gaps between strongpoints were covered by barbed wire, and sometimes AT ditches. The roads from the beaches were covered by the usual obstacles. There were also some strongpoints inland, usually based on artillery positions which added a little depth to the defence. The land defences may be compared to the Mareth Line, but the strength of that line, as with all defences, lay in the counter-attack, something the Rommelbelt would be found lacking.

The initial worry for the invaders was the difficulty in driving AFVs up the beach. The landing at Dieppe had shown that Churchills could bog down in shingle, and worse, it was found that some parts of the invasion beaches were blue clay which would usually bog tanks down, and certainly bog wheeled vehicles. Consequently the 'Bobbin' was developed. This was a huge roll of reinforced Hessian carpet wound round a reel carried across the front of an AVRE. When it was being laid the tank would drive along it. The carpet was designed for wheeled vehicles and was quickly destroyed if tanks drove on it. These bobbins were extensively deployed for the invasion which demonstrated how heavily the Dieppe experience was weighing on the planners minds.

The first task for the invaders in terms of crossing the beaches was to provide direct fire support. Naturally the RAF bombed the defences heavily before the invasion, although no accounts mention any ground attack during the fighting on the beaches, and the Navy also bombarded the defences. This weight of fire was not judged to be enough and it was decided to land some Shermans ahead of the other invading troops. This was achieved by providing the tanks with a flotation screen and a propeller driven by the tank's main engine. Such tanks were called 'DDs', Duplex-Drive tanks. Once these tanks were ashore the flotation screens were discarded and the tanks became ordinary gun tanks

The second task was to overcome the obstacles. These were of two kinds, underwater and on land. The underwater obstacles gave surprisingly little trouble, at least partly because the Germans had placed them under the assumption that the landing would take place at full tide, the actual landing was made well before that. There was a special RE unit organised to deal with them and there will be no further consideration of them here except to comment that the vast amount of labour used in their construction could have been employed much more profitably elsewhere.

The beach facing the troops as they landed was initially flat and open sand from three to five hundred yards deep. The first obstacle belt, just above the high water mark, was rows of steel AT obstacles, usually described as 'hedgehogs'.

Then, behind these came the dunes, some accounts call them 'sandbanks', a maximum of 100 yards deep, where the minefield was. Behind the dunes was the sea wall. There were German gun emplacements in front of the sea wall and along the lateral road that ran behind it. In front of the Queen Red landings, which will be considered below, was the large strongpoint WN 20 (*widerstandsnest 20*), codenamed COD. This strongpoint extended 600 yards along the sea wall, it included an 88-mm, 50-mm and a 47-mm gun each in a concrete emplacement, and a 50-mm gun in an open gun pit. There were two mortar positions, at least six MG posts and a 37-mm gun in a tank turret pillbox. There was also the full range of infantry weapons facing the invaders. Three of the assaulting specialised armour 'gapping' teams were to land opposite COD.

To overcome the obstacles the gapping teams had to cross the beach, under cover of fire from the DDs. Then they had to destroy the steel AT obstacles, and to do this they had Bangalore Torpedoes, After that they had to flail across the dunes, on rough going Mk 1 Crabs would take eight minutes to cover 100 yards, then the bridge and log carpet would be placed to provide a route over the sea wall. How all this worked will be considered in terms of Sword Beach.

To be correct SWORD was not the codename of the beach but of the force that was to attack it. The beach was QUEEN, and the important part of it was divided up into White and Red. However over the years the terms SWORD and QUEEN in this context have become interchangeable.

The QUEEN WHITE and RED beaches were not wide enough to land the two brigades side by side, so they had to land in tandem. To facilitate this as much as possible the Sword landing was given the maximum specialised armour support. This included two squadrons of AVREs, two squadrons of Crabs, and two squadrons of the DDs of the 13th/18th Royal Hussars.

The AVREs and Crabs were organised into gapping teams based on the RE troops, each of six AFVs, to be carried in a Landing Craft Tank (LCT). The mix of vehicles carried varied slightly for each team. There were eight gapping teams and two RE squadron reserves. The LCTs carrying the squadron reserves, which included armoured bulldozers, D7s, landed just after the gapping teams. At the insistence of the Navy the SBG bridges were loaded first so as to stand at the rear of the LCTs. The bridges tended to act as sails, and would deflect the craft least if stowed aft.

The gapping teams' LCTs were planned to arrive on the beach at 7.35am. The sea was rough on the morning of the invasion so the decision was made to launch the DDs from closer inshore, from 5,000 yards rather than 7,000. Thirty-two were launched, two were lost almost immediately but the crews were saved, and one was apparently run down by a LCT carrying AVREs and only the commander survived.

Because of the rough sea the DDs did not land a few minutes before the gapping teams as planned but at roughly the same time, this meant that they did not have the opportunity of beating down the German fire before the gapping teams arrived. When the DDs touched down, and blew off their screens, they naturally tended to stay in a few feet of water to present less of a target and not to risk any mines there might be on the beach. Unfortunately the following sea swamped nine of these tanks, leaving them immobile. They continued to provide fire support until their guns could no longer be loaded for water. One tank, from 'B' squadron, that did try to cross the beach was mined with such force that it was tipped on its side. The crew survived and in proper English fashion made a cup of tea!

Each of the gapping teams was allocated to a colour-coded gap. The gaps were planned to run up to roads pointing inland to ease exit from the beach, and in this they were generally successful. The progress of the gapping teams will be briefly considered below, running west to east.

77th Assault Squadron, RE
Green Gap, 1st Troop, with 3rd Troop, 'A' Sqn 22nd Dragoons.
The team consisted of three AVREs, bobbin, Log carpet and SBG bridge, and three Crabs.

Because the LCT was hit the AFVs disembarked a little earlier than planned, but this seems to have made no real difference except, though it may be unrelated to this, that there were no DDs there to give fire support. The Crabs flailed up to the sea wall and on to the lateral road. One AVRE, the bobbin, was hit by an AT gun while in the water, then apparently carrying on with one track, hit a mine. One of the sappers was killed while putting up a lane marker and the remainder of the crew continued as infantry. Apart from this one vehicle casualty the action was a success and the remaining AVREs proceeded west to assist with the fighting in Lion-sur-Mer where the troop leader was killed and both the AVREs became casualties.

Yellow Gap, 2nd Troop, with 3rd Troop, 'A' Sqn 22nd Dragoons.
The team consisted of four AVREs, GP, Log carpet, SBG bridge and bobbin, and two Crabs.

This team landed to the west of 1st Troop because its LCT drifted in the tide while it waited for the DDs to land, but it landed on time. The beach where the Yellow and Blue gaps were planned forms a small promontory jutting out into the sea only two to three hundred yards at low tide but probably enough to cause tides to deflect the Yellow and Blue gapping teams from their planned lanes. The first vehicle ashore, a Crab, saw a German gun to the west firing along the beach at the Green gapping team. The Crab charged it and ran over it. The only explanation for this event is that the Germans wheeled out a light AT gun, probably a 37-mm, down onto the beach, so to be able to enfilade the attackers. If it were a 37-mm it would have had little chance against Shermans and none against Churchills. If it were a 75-mm, as the regimental history claims, it is difficult to imagine it being man-handled like this, and difficult to imagine the Crab driving over it. A 37-mm would have been good enough for the light armour that the Germans would have anticipated landing. They were able to push the gun forward like this because there were no DDs here to drive them off. After this the Crab returned to more normal duties. Everything went well, though the Bangalore torpedo was exploded prematurely due to enemy fire, one Crab was mined, but the bridge was correctly dropped. The bobbin was damaged and jettisoned. The troop drove up the bridge onto the lateral road and joined 1st Troop in Lion-sur-Mer

Blue Gap, 3rd Troop, with 1st Troop, 'A' Sqn 22nd Dragoons. The team consisted of three AVREs, Log carpet, SBG bridge and bobbin, and three Crabs.

This team landed to the east of 4th Troop, presumably because of the general chaos. The LCT grounded on a submerged DD, so the AFVs had a rather greater drop into the water than they expected. The Crabs flailed up to the sea wall then the carpet and bridge were dropped and the troop got on to the lateral road. The bobbin was mined, hit by an AT gun, and drowned.

White Gap, 4th Troop, with 1st Troop, 'A' Sqn 22nd Dragoons.
The team consisted of four AVREs, Bullshorn plough, Log carpet, SBG bridge and bobbin, and two Crabs.

The LCT beached at the right place and time, the ramp dropped and the first Crab waded ashore. The second Crab was hit by AT fire and disabled, blocking the doorway. The

AVRE behind it was also disabled. There is some doubt but it is most likely that an AT gun was responsible for that as well. No further AFVs could be landed and the LCT returned to England. The rotating drum of the Crab that landed was shot off, so this tank functioned for the rest of the day as a gun tank.

The squadron reserve, consisting of two GP AVREs, two Crabs and an armoured bulldozer, followed 3rd Troop. It is not clear if they were involved in any fighting.

79th Assault Squadron, RE
Green Gap, 4th Troop, with 4th Troop, 'C' Sqn 22nd Dragoons.
The team consisted of four AVREs, GP, bobbin, Log carpet and SBG bridge, and two Crabs.

The AFVs landed on time and in the right place. One Crab was knocked out quite early, the other cleared the lane, but the bridge was badly placed, so the Crab flailed a second lane. The log carpet was correctly laid and the AFVs rallied on the lateral road. They proceeded to the lock gates in Ouistreham and stayed there until relieved by infantry.

Yellow Gap, 2nd Troop, with 4th Troop, 'C' Sqn 22nd Dragoons.
The team consisted of three AVREs, bobbin, Log carpet and SBG bridge, and three Crabs.

The AFVs landed on time and in the right place, but both Crabs were quickly knocked out, and the bridge fell prematurely, the release mechanism was hit be enemy fire. The lane was completed by hand and the exit from the beach was built up by a D7 armoured bulldozer after some of the sea wall was brought down by hand placed charges, an heroic action which cost the RE troop leader his life. Unfortunately all the AVREs were knocked out, which was predictable as this lane was directly in front of the strongpoint COD.

Blue Gap, 3rd Troop, with 3rd Troop, 'C' Sqn 22nd Dragoons. The team consisted of four AVREs, GP, bobbin, Log carpet and SBG bridge, and two Crabs.

The AFVs landed on time and in the right place, but both Crabs were quickly knocked out, and the lane was cleared by hand. The bridge was placed correctly but was later blocked by a DD tank falling off its side.

This troop was followed by the squadron reserve with two GP AVREs, two Crabs and two D7s. These reinforcements allowed a second lane to be flailed and an exit built up by a D7. The Crabs gamely attacked and destroyed two pillboxes that had caused the casualty in the Red gap.

Red Gap, 4th Troop, with 3rd Troop, 'C' Sqn 22nd Dragoons. The team consisted of three AVREs, bobbin, Log carpet and SBG bridge, and three Crabs.

The AFVs landed on time and in the right place, but one Crab was knocked out while still in the water by an AT gun, four of the crew were killed and the fifth badly injured. The other Crab cleared up to the dunes, the log carpet was laid and the AFVs got on to the lateral road.

As this brief account shows the gapping teams were generally successful in breaching the minefield and subduing German fire. They were, though, not totally successful and the following infantry took casualties on the beach, but mostly from indirect artillery fire that the gapping teams could do little about.

On a practical level it can be seen that the Bangalore torpedoes proved unnecessary. Not one was correctly used. In fact as they were carried on the outside of AVREs it may be that one contributed to the disaster to 4th Troop, 77th Assault Squadron. At least three teams jettisoned their Bangalore Torpedoes, no doubt high explosives on the outside of a tank was quite a worry! The bobbins were not used by Sword, and had very patchy success on other beaches.

The Crabs had performed well on the beaches. There is a worry with Crabs that, due to the weight of the flail, 3.3 tons, and this weight being badly distributed, they would bog down easily, but that did not happen. The flail did obscure the crew's vision and a Crab coming up from the beach is believed to have driven over ten to twelve wounded marines of 45th Commando, a kind of tragedy inseparable from armoured warfare.[1]

The success on Queen Beach may obscure the difficulties overcome, and it will be instructive to consider the assault of two of the inland strongpoints undertaken by two of the Sword units, but without Specialised Armour, a few hours after the landings.

HILLMAN
In general the tanks that moved off the beach were successful in their task of infantry support. Sometimes all did not go according to plan as the experiences of 'C' squadron 13th/18th Royal Hussars show [2]. This squadron was landed by LCT soon after the gapping teams and got off the beach hindered by nothing more than traffic jams. It joined the Suffolk regiment and they moved off to attack a defended battery codenamed MORRIS. The garrison surrendered almost immediately, yielding 67 prisoners, then the infantry and tanks attacked HILLMAN. This was a different story. HILLMAN was about two and a half miles inland covering an area of approximately 600 by 400 yards and it stands on slightly rising ground, this give it a view as far as the beaches but also made it vulnerable to naval gunfire. It consisted of 12 concrete emplacements, mostly

112

Tobruk shelters, some of which were accessed from larger bunkers. There were two command bunkers on the crest of the slope. They were fully underground and each contained five large rooms and a further five small ones for defence and anti-gas precautions. Each had a Tobruk by its entrance, and each had a tunnel about twenty yards long running forward to the base of a vertical shaft to an armoured cupola. It is impossible to be certain if these cupolas mounted machine guns or were for observation only. Probably the former as one who was there described them as turrets off old French tanks. Today the actual cupolas have long been taken for scrap iron, and one has been replaced by a mock-up. The Suffolks' account states that there were three cupolas, but the sites of only two can be positively identified.

To the rear of the two command bunkers on flatter ground was a shelter for two AT guns each in its separate casemate. This bunker was never completed and only one casemate was serviceable. Accounts say that there were two guns at HILLMAN and one was a 75-mm AT gun which would fill a casemate so the other must have been kept outside. The roof of this bunker was 3.5 meters of concrete thick, pretty-well indestructible.

HILLMAN was surrounded by two belts of barbed wire separated by a minefield about 40 yards thick containing both anti-tank and anti-personnel mines. The inner wire was about 50 yards in front of the cupolas. The minefield, and quite far beyond, was overlooked by the cupolas and several machine guns. Altogether HILLMAN looks far too elaborate to have been built as a part of Rommel's beach defence scheme. More likely its planned function, after being a regimental HQ, was to be an OP for the mobile batteries the Germans would have expected to deploy in line with their earlier, more mobile defensive scheme.

There were two main problems with HILLMAN from the attacker's point of view. The most important being that no-one had appreciated what a strong position it was. It had been believed to be a battalion HQ, but was actually the HQ of the 736th Coastal Defence Regiment and allocated a garrison of 150 men. On the next day, 7th June, 73 officers and men emerged from the underground bunkers to surrender. Also it was expected that it would have been neutralised by aerial and naval bombardment, but unfortunately the planes totally missed it, and the naval Forward Observation Officer became a casualty early on in the day so naval fire support did not materialise. On top of all this is it appears that its early capture was not regarded as particularly urgent. This is shown by a visit by the divisional commander who merely commented that HILLMAN should be taken by dark to allow time for digging in. The scene, then, was set for some difficult fighting, which would illustrate the growing importance of mines as AT weapons.

The attack began at 1.00pm supported by a heavy barrage of HE and smoke from the Shermans. As the magnitude of the task was not fully appreciated the attack was to be carried out by a single company reinforced by a 'breaching' platoon which would use the Bangalore torpedoes. The attack was put in from the north as this was the first point reached from the coast, and there was some corn there that gave some cover. The outer perimeter wire was breached and two RE teams of two men each working lying flat on the ground cleared a 'sheep track' to the inner perimeter wire. Until now the defenders had not opened fire but when a platoon moved up to the wire and blasted it with a Bangalore torpedo, it was halted by intense MG fire.

Despite the smoke there can be no doubt that the Bangalore had alerted the defenders as to the exact location of the breach, and it was only 50 yards from the nearest cupola. The gap could be fired on by two cupolas, probably five

Tobruks, and the garrisons of dozens if not hundreds of yards of trenches. The first two men to try to go through the gap were killed, but a PIAT group was moved up, it fired three bombs at the nearest cupola without any apparent effect. Other soldiers managed to capture a Tobruk shelter and two of its occupants. Although at least another platoon got through the wire no further progress was made, this might be due to the fact that the company commander and another officer had been killed.

While this was happening the tanks had moved up to the outer perimeter where one was hit, but not disabled, by an AT gun, but even from there their direct fire could not knock out the MGs that were holding up the attack. The Tobruks were very difficult to subdue. They were cleverly sited on the rising ground, just out of the attackers' sight. This however did mean that their view of the attackers was obscured by long grass, probably the main reason why any attackers survived at all. The defender would fire a few rounds then duck down leaving the tanks with nothing to fire at. The problem was made worse by the defenders not firing tracer. The steel cupola that was causing most of the trouble was hit several times by 17-pdr AP shot, and was certainly neutralised. It totally dominated the area attacked and no-one could have survived there if it was still firing.

The Suffolk's CO concluded that no progress could be made within the inner perimeter without the support of tanks, so he ordered the troops that had penetrated that far to withdraw while the tanks continued their firing. His problem was that the infantry could not advance due to MG fire, because of the design of the fortifications the tanks and artillery could not subdue the MGs, and the tanks could not advance because of the mines.

There followed something of an impasse while the Suffolk's CO organised the next move to cope with the challenge that Hillman had turned out to be. This impasse lasted about four hours. Mines were the main problem and to make a passage for tanks was a much more difficult task than making a track for infantry, so he got two flail tanks ordered up. Fortunately he did not wait for them as they did not arrive until a breach had been made. Also a squadron of Staffordshire Yeomanry was ordered up, but was soon ordered away before taking any part in the fighting, it being required elsewhere. Then he ordered the RE detachment to make greater efforts to widen the sheep track to make a route for tanks. This was a much greater undertaking. A sheep track can, with luck, be made just by marking mines, but a passage for tanks involves lifting or detonating a large number of mines. The engineers set to with gelignite charges. Interestingly the engineers found themselves clearing old British Mark 75 Hawkins mines left behind at Dunkirk.

Slowly the fire of the tanks began to prevail. One troop (four tanks) which had been sent round to the east to reconnoitre some probable German positions came under AT gun fire, probably from HILLMAN, and lost two tanks, the others were recalled. This increased the weight of fire and the AT gun was knocked out. It was in an open emplacement, the gun having been wheeled out of the shelter, and one gunner was in front of it pulling the gun round, presumable after engaging the tanks to the east. He was hit and his body hung grotesquely across the barrel. A MG post was also knocked out. As soon as the engineers could predict a 50/50 chance of clearance the squadron said it was ready to try and the order to attack was given. The commander of the point tank was reluctant to advance as he would have driven over an infantryman's corpse, but a short discussion with an infantry NCO changed his mind and the attack went in and succeeded in capturing the main defences. A flail tank did turn up but the breach was already made.

Once the attackers were through the minefield the tanks could give support to the infantry in the usual way although initially the tanks advanced too fast for the infantry. They were called back and the attack ran smoothly. The tank commanders helped by attacking the Germans in the trenches with grenades. The tanks went right through the position to cut off any retreating defenders. While making this move the Squadron Leader's tank was lost in bizarre circumstances. It suddenly disappeared. It had driven over the roof of a large underground bunker, and the roof gave away under the tank's weight. The squadron war diary describes this bunker as the officers' latrine, which no doubt evoked many humorous comments at the time, but a visit to the site gives the impression that it is more likely that it was a munitions store and water tank.

The fighting was over by 8.15pm, but the German commander in his underground command post did not surrender until around midnight. He was in contact by telephone with his superiors right to the end. The attackers had lost two officers and five ORs killed and about eight ORs wounded.

There is no doubt that HILLMAN held out much longer than it should have. It is difficult to judge how important this was in the big picture of the failure to capture Caen on the first day, but on a smaller scale the consequences were terrible. Another infantry battalion came under the fire of HILLMAN's MGs and suffered around 40 casualties. This would not have happened if HILLMAN had been taken on time.

The assault of HILLMAN showed how important tanks were for infantry support, and how, in they were held up by mines, the attack would stall. Crabs, and specialised armour in general, from now on became an integral part of the planning for the assault of any prepared defence.

Notes:
1. This story keeps recurring, for example see www.hitlernews.cloudworth.com/british-tanks.php, and it is hard to believe it is not true, but it is difficult to pin down in history.
2. In his well-known book, 'The Noble Duke of York', Lt-Col AH Burne wrote "*Whether history repeats itself may be a matter of doubt, but there can be no doubt that the gibe is true that historians repeat one another.*" This is particularly true of those writing about the capture of HILLMAN. Since the publication of 'Assault Division', by Norman Scarfe, in 1947 most accounts of the Normandy campaign, even modern ones, credit the action to the Staffordshire Yeomanry and ignore the 13th/18th Royal Hussars. Hopefully the account given here will redress to balance to some degree.

Operation Astonia
The Capture of Le Havre

After the Normandy battles had been brought to a close and the German forces had fallen back almost out of France, a number of the Channel ports were still holding out and had to be taken by assault. Le Havre was the most important of these ports. Its fourteen basins and eight miles of quays were needed by the Allies who were already experiencing logistic problems, so its capture was a matter of urgency. It had a large garrison, believed at the time to be 8,700 but which actually turned out to be 12,000. Fortunately the defences were nowhere near as good as they were believed to be, and there was a shortage of anti-tank guns, the Normandy battles having taken priority for them.

The German Defences
The shape of the defended area of Le Havre was a rough square and the northern face was its most vulnerable. Its western and southern faces were covered by the sea and the Seine, and the eastern face by the Lezarde river. The northern face was defended by field works. Behind the town and port of Le Havre the ground rises sharply and the high ground forms two plateaux, the northern and the southern, divided by the Fontaine river. The field works ran

across the northern plateau. The eastern 2000 yards of the northern front were selected for the attack and will be described below. *(See Sketch 4)*

On the map it may seem that there was a case for making the Fontaine the main obstacle. It was certainly a good obstacle though the approach to it was very steep, broken and heavily wooded. It would have been difficult to defend it against infantry. The main reason it was not used was that the Germans had already built Strongpoint 8 just to the east of the village of Fontaine La Mallet. This strongpoint contained some impressively strong concrete gun emplacements, and it appears that the long term plan had been to build a series of such strongpoints across the northern front. There was certainly one on the western side of Fontaine La Mallet. The front, then, had to link Strongpoint 8 with the Lezarde. The implication is that there were two defensive schemes, one being the long term unfinished scheme which produced the concrete emplacements, and the later one being the emergency scheme, which produced the other defences.

The land to the west of Strongpoint 8 is broken and hilly, but between Strongpoint 8 and the Lezarde it is flat and open. There is a small stream running roughly eastwards from the strongpoint. The land slopes gently down to it for about 200 yards on each side. The plateau to the north and south of this slight depression is the same elevation as Strongpoint 8 which flanks the stream very effectively. This stream was very important because, even though it was an insignificant obstacle, crossing it resulted in exposure to fire from Strongpoint 8 and the ground close to the stream would dry out more slowly than that on the rest of the plateau, slowing the tanks down at the critical time.

The defences had three main elements; an AT ditch, minefields and strongpoints.

The central feature was the AT ditch. It was of 'V' cross section, 22 feet wide at the top and 4 feet wide at the bottom, and 12 feet nine inches deep. It was not continuous and on the 49th West Riding Division front only one of the three attacks had to cross it. The trace of the ditch is now totally lost. The land here is intensively farmed and any sign of it was ploughed out, or built on, long ago. To the east of Strongpoint 8 it was dug to be close to the top of the southern slope down to the stream. This was the front to be attacked by the 49th WR Division. The depth of the minefield in front of the ditch is not known but 500 yards was allowed for. It would be reasonable to assume that the minefield covered the sloping ground, and this was a maximum of 500 yards.

There was a gap in the ditch close to Strongpoint 8, probably because the stream here was a good enough obstacle, then it ran around Strongpoint 8 well to its north. On this section, which was to be attacked by the 51st Highland Division, the minefield was behind the ditch. Presumably, because this section was on almost the same elevation as Strongpoint 8 the minefield, being more difficult to cover by fire, was laid closer.

There were 14 strongpoints on the assaulted front. Most are now lost, but Strongpoint 5, being right behind the minefield and the second most tactically important, is still extant. As can be seen the German defence depended on the AT obstacle, and there was no real attempt to set up two defensive belts, the advanced position and the main line, as their manuals demanded, examples of which the Guards tanks had to fight through at Caumont. This can be regarded as a basic difference between fortress and field fortifications.

Even the finest defences lose a large percentage of their value if their exact nature and position are known by the attackers, and this was the case at Le Havre. Not only had they been extensively photographed by the RAF but many deserters and Frenchmen had supplied all kinds of detailed information.

The weak points of these defences, as with many others, lay with the lack of determination of the commander and the poor morale of the garrison. The commander, Colonel Wildemuth, was, despite Hitler's exhortations, realistically pessimistic about the defence. The main reason for his pessimism was that the garrison consisted of poor quality troops, who were described by one of their commanders as *'fortress troops, sailors, home guards, harbour technicians and stragglers'*, and they were well aware of their strategic situation, hopelessly cut off. They had been subjected to several nights of bombing, the final raid was on the strongpoints and judged, by British observers, to be accurate and effective. This was followed by an artillery pounding, so perhaps it was not too surprising that many defenders surrendered as soon as the attacking tanks were through the minefields. Certainly there was no counter-attack, which was not surprising as the garrison had no armoured vehicles, and not even an instance of a tank being attacked with a panzerfaust. All in all the defences were not that formidable, but they certainly seemed so to the attackers.

The Assault
The responsibility for the left flank of the advancing Allied forces, from Le Havre to Bruges fell to the 1st Canadian Army, and the task of reducing Le Havre fell to 1st British Corps (i.e. not a Canadian unit). This corps contained two divisions, the 49th and the 51st, each of which were to provide a brigade for the assault. These two brigades, the 56th and the 152nd, would receive extensive support from two armoured brigades and from specialised armour provided by the 79th Division. The scope of this support may be shown by a list of the main infantry and armoured units involved:

1st Corps, Lt Gen JT Crocker
    49th West Riding Division, Maj Gen EH Barker
        56th Brigade
            2nd South Wales Borderers
            2nd Gloucestershire Regiment
            2nd Essex Regiment
            Under command, from 79th Armoured Division
            222nd Assault Squadron RE (AVREs)
            22nd Dragoons, two squadrons (Crabs)
            141 RAC, one squadron (Crocodiles)
        146th Brigade
        147th Brigade
        under command
        34th Armoured Brigade (Churchills)
            7 RTR
            9 RTR
            107 RAC
            147 RAC
            1st Canadian Armoured Personnel Carrier
            Squadron (44 Kangaroos)
    51st Highland Division, Maj Gen TG Rennie
        152nd Brigade
            2nd and 5th Seaforth Highlanders
            5th Queens Own Cameron Highlanders
            under command, from 79th Armoured Division
            16th Assault Squadron RE (AVREs)
            1st Lothian and Border Yeomanry, one squadron
            (Crabs)
            141 RAC, one squadron (Crocodiles)
        153rd Brigade
        154th Brigade
        under command
        33rd Armoured Brigade (Shermans)
            1st Northamptonshire Yeomanry
            East Riding Yeomanry
            144 RAC

Le Havre could have been attacked on two fronts, the eastern, based on the river Lezarde, or the northern. The Lezarde had been dammed close to the sea to build up substantial inundations, just as had been done for the siege of 1415, and it was overlooked by both the northern and southern plateaux. Clearly an attack on this front would be infantry based, possibly resulting in heavy casualties, and could not be expected to yield dramatic results due to the small number of roads for the follow up. On the other hand an attack on the northern front would be tank based, the specialized armour necessary being available in large numbers. The casualties would be fewer, and a breakthrough here would be easier to follow up.

The resulting Corps plan was in four phases:

Phase I   The 49th WR Division would break through the defences on the northern front, capture the strongpoints to its south and cross the Fontaine.

Phase II   i) The 51st Highland Division would break through to the right of the 49th Division's breach, and capture the strongpoints in that vicinity.
ii) 49th Division to capture the southern plateau.

Phase III   51st Division to secure German defences around Octeville, and the high ground directly to the north of Le Havre.

Phase IV 'Ruthless exploitation into the town to take advantage of any early enemy weakness'.

Progressively, from the 2nd September, forces had been taking up position around Le Havre and it was soon surrounded. The town and defences were subject to a nearly continual pounding by Bomber Command. This was judged to have lowered the morale of the defenders but did not cause significant damage to the defences. It did result in the deaths of approximately 5,000 French civilians. That the defenders were not enthusiastic is shown by the capture, on 3rd September, of an entire company by a reconnaissance unit. The attackers, though, were hampered by continual and depressing rain. The attack was originally scheduled for the 9th but the ground was so soft that it was put back to the 10th. The rain stopped and a drying wind sprang up but even so there were plenty of misgivings about the state of the ground. Unfortunately the attack could not be postponed again as the AVREs were required elsewhere, which shows how important specialised armour had become.

The artillery support was prodigious. It was provided by eight field regiments, six medium regiments, and one heavy regiment, being respectively 25-pdr, 5.5-inch and 155-mm guns. Also a number of 3.7-inch HAA guns were used. The total was 370 guns.

As will be seen from the names of the lanes, through the minefields there was to be no attempt to indicate them at night with hurricane lamps inside tins with easily recognisable symbols cut out, as was done at Alamein with the 'Sun', 'Moon' and other lanes. It is impossible now to tell if this omission had any bad effects.

The 49th WR Division's Attack
The 56th Brigade had the most important role in the battle which was to penetrate the northern defences as far as the Fontaine, and establish crossings. The 147th Brigade would exploit beyond that. The initial attack would be assisted by a demonstration by the 51st Division in front of Octeville. The 146th Brigade was to make a secondary attack from the east across the Lezarde.

The 56th Brigade's Attack

The objectives of the brigade's attack were to be achieved in two phases. In phase 1a in the corps plan it would cross the minefield and, where necessary, the AT ditch. In phase 1b it would capture Strongpoints 1 to 7 (including 2a, now lost), and cross the Fontaine.

The initial attack, timed to start at 5.45pm, was to be on a two battalion front. The 2nd Glosters on the left and the 2nd South Wales Borderers (SWB) on the right. The minefield would be breached by the Crabs of the 22nd Dragoons. The 2nd Essex, mounted on Kangaroos, would follow through the assaulting units on towards the Fontaine. Kangaroos were disarmed Priest self-propelled guns used as armoured personnel carriers and will be considered in the next chapter.

Phase 1a
The move to the forming up position, which was in dead ground around 3,000 yards north east of the AT ditch to be attacked, took place on the night of 9th/10th September. This move was a very complex undertaking involving around 130 tracked armoured vehicles plus two battalions of infantry but excluding a battalion in Kangaroos that would have formed up behind the main body. All these vehicles required ammunition and fuel, and 300 tons of stores had been moved forward. The muddy condition of the ground caused difficulties particularly for the bridgelayers and Crabs. Of the latter, they being prone to bogging down, only two troops managed the move overnight and the remainder, nearly two squadrons, moved up during the day covered by a smoke screen. Some were dragged by AVREs.

The Commanding Officer of the 22nd Dragoons was perturbed by the effect which the sodden ground would have on the efficiency of flailing. He was doubtful if a speed of 1 mph, which would produce the 1500 revs considered the minimum necessary for flailing, could be reached. His worries were justified as only 900 to 1400 revs were achieved, which resulted in many mines not being exploded.

The aerial bombardment started at 4.15pm. Many tank crews closed down when they heard the planes coming, they had had experience of being accidentally bombed during the Normandy campaign. The waiting infantry just watched. The bombing was very accurate and 4,600 tons were dropped on the strongpoints. It was believed to have been very effective, but only the bombing of Strongpoints 1, 5 and 8 could have been properly observed, the land being so flat.

The attack started at 5.45pm with an artillery bombardment, which concentrated on the strongpoints for 115 minutes then switched to other targets. There was an arrangement in the fire plan to switch back to the strongpoints if necessary. Also smoke was laid just in front of the minefield. The weather was cold and clear.

Each lane was attacked by a gapping team which consisted in most cases of a troop of Crabs followed by AVREs, each lane had its own commander.

At 6.15 the Crabs crossed the start line (codename BETTY). They did not initially come under much fire. The left hand troop was fired on by an 88-mm Pak 43/41 in an open position in Strongpoint 1, and, as they had not yet started flailing they could return fire and silenced it. Normally Shermans in the open would stand little chance against an 88 and it may be suspected that in this case its crew was suffering from the effect of the bombardment.

Fifteen minutes after the Crabs crossed the start line they were followed by two squadrons of Churchills of 7RTR. At roughly the same time the Crabs crossed the flailing line (codename JUDY) which was roughly 500 yards in front of the AT ditch, and started flailing.

The move forward to the flailing line did not go totally smoothly. It involved passing through a slight bottleneck of about a quarter of a mile's width. The assaulting team for the centre gap (HAZEL) started 10 minutes later than the others. The ground was reduced to a mass of muddy tank tracks, and the marking posts had been knocked down, so these Crabs, and the following AVREs and bridgelayer, lost direction. The 30th Armoured Brigade that supplied the AVREs was rather critical of the tanks, saying that there was a '*mass of 'I' tanks milling around in the bottleneck*'. It is just possible that the tanks were jockeying for better firing positions because of the smoke screen and the dust thrown up by the flails. Whatever the cause was, the start of flailing in this gap was delayed a few minutes.

One of the hazards risked by the AFV commanders was Rommel's Asparagus. This was a series of poles driven into the ground as obstacles against gliders. Barbed wire was strung criss-cross between the tops of these poles and this was a danger to any tank commander looking out of his cupola. This may have made navigation that bit more difficult, and as the attack progressed so mortar and machine gun fire from the right flank became more intense causing many casualties among the SWB and dismounted tank crews.

The Crabs were to flail three gaps through the minefield. These were named, from the west, LAURA, HAZEL and MARY. Each gap was to be of two or three lanes and each lane would require a troop of five Crabs and be three tank-widths wide, 24 feet. The exception to this rule was the centre HAZEL lane, this was to be along a sunken track which had been reported as not mined so needed no Crabs. The control of a flailing Crab presented certain difficulties mostly due to dust and a wash/wipe system was developed for periscopes not dissimilar to that on modern car headlights. The leading Crab had, above each of its rear idlers, two arms holding lamps, to keep following Crabs on station. Crabs marked the flailed ground by firing, with small cartridges, rods into the ground.

Progress on the gaps.
LAURA
Right lane. Crabs in this gap came under AT gunfire from Strongpoint 8, and naturally the weight of this fire fell on this lane. The leading Crab was soon hit, its turret was blown off and the entire crew were casualties. The second Crab was blown up on a mine, but fortunately in a location hidden from the gun. The remaining three were through the minefield at 7.01pm, but just at that moment the troop leader's Crab was hit and burst into flames. The entire crew was killed. The two surviving Crabs turned round to widen the lane. One was blown up, but the other reached the start line, the lane was complete at 20 feet by 7.28.

Centre lane. Three Crabs blown up, first through at 7.05, lane complete at 24 feet by 7.26.

Left lane. Two Crabs were blown up and one hit by AT gunfire from Strongpoint 8. The first Crab was through at 7.10 and by 7.33 the lane was 12 feet wide. The Crab hit by gunfire was, at 7.30, burned out by an advancing Crocodile, fortunately the crew had already abandoned it. No further details of this event have been found.

Total vehicle casualties were three Crabs burned out, nine Crabs and one Sherman command tank disabled either by mines or gunfire. There was no AT ditch here to cross. This gap ran right up to Strongpoint 5, and the lack of serious resistance here was a testament to the effectiveness of the bombing.

HAZEL
This gap involved crossing the AT ditch. This was to be done by SBG bridges and a Churchill bridgelayer,

presumably because the ditch was too deep to be crossed on fascines, and because of the requirement to move wheeled vehicles forward which could not negotiate fascines. The centre lane, being along an existing track and so expected to carry most traffic, was to be spanned by the Churchill bridgelayer. The AFVs, except the bridgelayer, were from 222 Assault Squadron RE. There were either two SBG bridges, or the bridgelayer and an SBG bridge, per lane, one of the SBG bridges would be kept back initially as a reserve in the dead ground of the forming up position.

Flailing started a few minutes late due to the Crabs losing direction on the approach. The right lane was flailed to a three-vehicle width by 7.30pm but due to the delay in starting flailing the SBG bridge was all but stationary in the open for 30 minutes, and as German fire increased the bridge was hit by mortar fire and dropped. A Snake, which was a variant of a Bangalore torpedo, but which could reach further, was also hit and exploded. The Snakes were used so that the Crabs would not have to flail right up to the edge of the AT ditch. The reserve SBG bridge was called forward but when about 500 yards from the ditch the bridge fell, probably crossing a road, the winch brakes had failed. The bridge's crew dismounted and spent 20 minutes, under heavy fire, winching it back up and lashing it in position. They were covered by smoke put down by an AVRE while they carried out this task.

The troop leader led the SBG bridge forward, taking a chance on the possibility of unexploded mines close to the AT ditch, and controlled the lowering of the bridge. He crawled forward and checked it, and at 8.55pm reported it as complete. Unfortunately two infantry carriers bogged down in the lane, which was by now very muddy, and blocked the lane until 3.00am.

The central lane was intended to run down a sunken track. It had been reported as not mined so the Churchill bridgelayer moved off 15 minutes after the other teams. When it did so it was held up by the melee of tanks in the bottleneck, and was held back until this had sorted itself out. When it did move forward it hit a mine losing three bogies (roadwheels) and breaking a track. This completely blocked the sunken track. Later that night the track was swept up to the bridgelayer with mine detectors, possibly by the divisional RE but, as AVREs often carried mine detectors, the crews could have done this themselves. Then an AVRE was backed up to it to tow it out so that a SBG bridge could be brought up, but the AVRE also went up on a mine. The track was swept again, but soon after a scout car was blown up. It was later discovered that some mines had been buried deep and were exploded by vertical rods that had only two or three inches showing above the ground. Mine detectors missed these.

The bridgelayer was finally got up to the AT ditch but then the bridge could not be dropped, presumably the mechanism had been damaged by the mine blast. The bridgelayer and AVRE were pulled back and the AT ditch bulldozed in and the lane cleared by 3.00pm next day.

The Left lane was a disaster. It was difficult for the Crabs because of the standing corn which had a cushioning effect reducing the flails' efficiency, and all five Crabs were soon disabled. Consequently the lane commander ordered the Snake forward. It was brought up in the troop leader's AVRE which was followed by another AVRE which was to push it, but the latter went up on a mine. Then the SBG bridge hit a mine and the bridge, damaged by mortar fire, fell across the lane.

The troop leader started to push the Snake forward, it buckled so he went forward and straightened it, he then pushed it into position and fired it. Unfortunately after this achievement his AVRE went up on a mine. The lane was then abandoned. The next day this troop leader, sweeping up to his AVRE, picked up eight AT mines.

MARY

There was no AT ditch here.

The right lane. One Crab got through by 7.08pm, but by 7.47 the lane was entirely blocked by Crabs or tanks that had hit mines.

The left lane. By 7.08 a 24 feet lane had been flailed and three AVREs, four crocodiles and two troops of B squadron 7RTR passed through. Then two tanks hit mines and the lane was blocked until 8.28pm.

Throughout the next two days vehicles would be going up on deep laid mines, so the state of the lanes was subject to some variation, but at 8.15am on 11th September it was:

LAURA	1	Right,	lane in use
	2	Centre,	blocked
	3	Left,	blocked
HAZEL	4	Right,	expected to be ready for 9.00am
	5	Centre,	blocked by bridgelayer
	6	Left,	abandoned.
MARY	7	Right,	blocked
	8	Left,	available for tanks only

Because of the sodden state of the ground it was soon only crossable by tracked vehicles or on foot. It is remarkable that the German artillery was not more effective against the lanes, particularly those depending on bridges. Perhaps the Germans had fewer guns than sources imply, and most of the fire coming down was from mortars. Counter-battery fire was judged not to be as effective as usual because the German gunners had concrete shelters.

Tank casualties seemed very heavy, next day the minefield was said to look like '*a park for damaged tanks*'. The 22nd Dragoons had lost 29 flails out of 33, and two command tanks, the 222nd Assault squadron, five AVREs, and 7RTR, six tanks. However, the vast majority of these casualties were on mines and reasonably easy to repair.

The 22nd Dragoons only recorded 11 tanks as either total losses or beyond local repair, these being: one burned out by Crocodile, two struck by shells from a 75-mm AT gun, seven damaged by mines or HE shells, and one with a mechanical defect in gearbox.

Phase 1b
This phase was a continuation of 1a. The battalion on the right, the SWB, had as objectives Strongpoints 5, 6 and 7. It was supported by half a squadron of Crocodiles from 141 Regiment RAC, and a troop of AVREs from 1st troop, 617 Assault Squadron RE.

The plan was for two AVREs to pass through each of the LAURA lanes, but only three made it. One struck a mine, one was hit in the transmission by an 88-mm AT gun, and one was jammed in between a knocked out tank and a carrier. The three crews spent the night carrying infantry casualties back under heavy fire.

Two Crocodiles were knocked out on the start line. On Crocodiles the link between the fuel trailer and the tank itself was very vulnerable to threats like mortar fire that the tank was proof against. This may have caused these losses. Another Crocodile was knocked out passing through the minefield, leaving six able to flame.

The AVREs and the Crocodiles were vital to the attack. The strongpoints themselves were easily captured as the garrisons did not put up much of a fight, in fact 40 German soldiers were captured sheltering in the underground bunker of Strongpoint 5. However the infantry of the SWB suffered heavily from fire from Strongpoint 8. Because of this the four AFVs outran their infantry support and arrived on the last objective, Strongpoint 7, an hour in front of the infantry. *En route* the AVREs knocked out an 88, hitting it from a flank. The strongpoint was secure at 10.40pm.

Strongpoint 8 was one of the 51st Highland Division's objectives, and it would not be attacked for some time. To compensate for this it had been hit by 600 rounds of HE and 1200 mortar smoke rounds (to blind searchlights), but was still showing plenty of fight. However the strongpoints were, in general, not mined and the defenders had nothing to fight against the AVREs and crocodiles with.

The left battalion, 2nd Glosters, carried out a very impressive attack. It crossed the start line at 7.00pm. There was fairly heavy fire coming down to the north of the minefield but little, if any to the south. 'D' company crossed through MARY left lane, which was opened at 7.08, and they overran Strongpoint 1 at 7.20pm. This strongpoint was so close to the minefield that one of the Crabs fell into one of its trenches.

The battalion was supported by half a squadron of Crocodiles and a troop of AVREs (3rd Troop). The plan was for half the vehicles of each unit to use each of the two MARY lanes. Unfortunately the right lane failed and the AFVs trying to use this lane were redirected to the left. These AFVs crossed the minefield too late for the Glosters' battle.

Because of the difficulty with the right lane 'B' and 'C' companies followed 'D' through the left. So there was a delay in capturing Strongpoint 2a which was done at 7.40. The plan was for 'A' company to follow seven minutes later with a troop each of Crocodiles and AVREs, but there was a delay in the lane when only a part of 'A' company had passed through. However the troops of Crocodiles and AVREs and some tanks were through so these, with a mixed party of parts of 'A' and 'B' companies went forward into the smoke to carry out 'A' company's orders. Unfortunately they lost direction and spent some time flaming and firing at the west and south sides of Strongpoint 3 under the impression it was 2a. Then they went on and captured Strongpoints 9 and 10. They withdrew when they realised their mistake.

The AVREs were very effective, scoring a direct hit on a concrete post with a petard at a range of 80 yards. They also claimed an 88, as did the Crabs flailing the MARY gap.

Meanwhile the remainder of 'A' company, supported by Crocodiles, captured Strongpoint 2a, but lost their company commander who died of wounds. There was then a pause for reorganisation. Following this 'A' company captured Strongpoint 3, with three German officers and 25 ORs. 'B' company moved to the right of 'A' company, 'C' passed through them and took Strongpoint 4, with one officer and 22 ORs, at 9.18pm. At 10.45 2nd Essex passed through. This eventful action cost the lives of one officer and one OR, and 22 ORs were wounded.

Phase 1c
The 2nd Essex were to capture Strongpoints 9 and 10, clear the remainder of the northern plateau and establish a bridgehead on the southern plateau in the north eastern part of the Foret de Montgeon.

The plan was for the battalion to travel in Kangaroos to the area captured by the Glosters, then proceed on foot. They did the move to the minefield mounted, thereby saving possible casualties from mortar and machine gun fire, but the Commanding Officer judged that the state of the gaps was so bad that he ordered the battalion to dismount and advance on foot. He only took three vehicles, the rear link radio, RA radio and 7RTR Liaison vehicles, and these used HAZEL and not MARY as originally planned. The accompanying AVREs of 2nd troop did, though, pass through the minefield. The move through the minefield was ordered at 9.30.

Once through 'C' company was left as a reserve by Strongpoint 1, and 'A' and 'B' companies were sent, each with a troop of tanks, to capture Strongpoints 9 and 10 respectively. This could not have been much of a challenge as both had already been captured once by the Glosters, and both were duly reported as secure by 12.30am.

The infantry had not needed AVRE support for this task so the AVRE troop proceeded with its prearranged engineering tasks. Half the troop went down the steep (40 degrees) slope to the south of Strongpoint 10 down to the road (now Avenue de Mendes France). The distance was around 50 yards and the AVREs were led on foot by the Squadron Commander even though there was a danger from anti-personnel 'S' mines. Their task was to destroy two roadblocks. They were around 300 yards apart and the AVREs came onto the road between them. Both of these roadblocks consisted of two concrete walls four feet thick with a crater in between. The AVREs drove up to the northern one. The walls were destroyed by demolition charges (200 lbs of 808, the standard TNT-like demolition explosive). Then the AVREs moved south and destroyed the second. A bulldozer belonging to the divisional RE was brought up to fill in the craters and nearly finished the job before going up on a mine at the second roadblock. The job was finally complete at 9.00am next day when a second dozer became available.

The other half troop proceeded to the Fontaine and constructed two crossings using chespale (chestnut paling) and culverting towed forward on sledges. Even though the Essex captured two bridges these crossings were very useful. This troop took with it an SBG bridge. It covered 6,000 yards at half a mile an hour throughout the night led

135

by a Lance Corporal on a motor bike. This was an achievement, particularly considering the steep drop down to the Fontaine. Unfortunately within 100 yards of that river it hit a couple of bumps and fell. Fortunately it was not needed, and if it had been no doubt it could have been dragged into place.

A platoon from each of 'A' and 'C' companies had been sent to capture the two bridges over the Fontaine, which they did, but the CO decided he did not have sufficient manpower to advance into the Foret de Montgeon.

Phase II
The 51st Highland Division's attack
The division consisted of three brigades, 152nd, 153rd and 154th. The initial assault on the German defences would be carried out by the 152nd Brigade, 153rd would pass through 152nd when its objectives had been taken, and 154th was kept back for exploitation.

The German defences to be attacked were slightly different from those attacked by the 49th Division. The AT ditch was in front of the minefield, and behind the minefield was Strongpoint 8 on slightly higher ground. The division used the German numbers and called it Strongpoint 76. This position so dominated the minefield that it was judged impossible to breach it in daylight but as the division had to have gaps of its own, it could not expect to use 49th Division's, so it was decided to make the gaps at night. The divisional attack would be in the opposite sequence to 49th Division's, first the strongpoints, then the gaps. Crossing the AT ditch and breaching the minefield at night was a very ambitious task but could be risked because the Highland Division's attack was secondary to the 49th Division's. To assist the attack a diversion was arranged in the Octeville area, but it is not known how important, or effective, it was.

The first action was to commence at 11.00pm when the 5th Seaforths would cross the minefield through gap LAURA, or HAZEL if necessary, form up in Strongpoint 5, then assault Strongpoint 76. Gapping would start at roughly the same time.

This battalion carried out its orders almost to the letter. Strongpoint 5 was taken as the start line for the attack and the move through the minefield as the approach march. This approach march was very difficult. A little light was generated by shining some searchlights on the clouds. This was known as 'Monty's moonlight'. The lanes were very muddy, some tank tracks being two feet deep, but this was not entirely a bad thing as they did offer crawling soldiers some protection against artillery. At least some of the battalion must have passed through HAZEL because the Regimental History mentions an SBG bridge over the AT ditch and LAURA did not cross a ditch. The battalion formed up at the start line in good time.

During this move the battalion had suffered heavy casualties from German artillery. It was particularly unlucky in this respect, since up to this point the German artillery had not been very effective against the gaps. Although a counter-battery programme was being carried out, once again it was not as effective as hoped because of the protection offered to the German gunners by their concrete bunkers.

At 12.40am the leading company, 'C' company, started its attack, glad to escape the shelling. They immediately found proof of the low morale of the defenders. Their first objective was a pillbox about 500 yards to the west. A communications trench had been dug right up to it, and this trench was empty except for a Pole who seemed to be loitering with intent to desert. He led the company up to the pillbox which was a dummy. This trench ran along behind the front line and now the company turned north-east to approach the rear of Strongpoint 76. Their second task was to breach the wire behind the strongpoint but this had already been done by the artillery. Now 'D' company passed through 'C' to attack the strongpoint. Their approach was difficult as the night was very dark and the map gave no indication of the steep climb they came to. However as they reached the top they were in Strongpoint 76 and the garrison, with almost no resistance, gave itself up.

The strongpoint contained two 88s, one 75, one 50-mm, and the dug-in turret of a Czech tank mounting a 45-mm. There were two 20-mm AA guns, some banks of rockets waiting to be fired, and eighty men. There were some mines but the company luckily missed them. The company was then heavily shelled so the defenders must have been in telephone communications with their HQ when the position was captured, which occurred at 3.00am.

The other companies all took their objectives, which were locations close to Strongpoint 76, almost without opposition. Next morning brought in many prisoners. This action cost the battalion 20 dead and 30 wounded.

Crossing the AT ditch and Minefield
As there were no mines to the north of the AT ditch the Crabs were not required until the ditch had been crossed so the attack was to be led by AVREs. The leading one carried the snake that would be launched across the AT ditch to clear any mines on the opposite side. The next vehicle, in the centre lane only, was a Crab because it carried a gyroscopic compass, and was needed for direction keeping. Then came an SBG bridge. These were backed up by AVREs carrying fascines.

There were to be three lanes, lanes one, two and three, or codenames GIN, RUM and ALE. A little light would be provided by Monty's 'moonlight', and direction would be kept by a Bofors gun firing trace above the middle lane. The AVREs would cross the start line at 12.10am 11th September. The start line was 2,000 yards away from the AT ditch, it had been planned for this distance to be crossed in 40 minutes, but actually it took an hour. The lanes were to be about two hundred yards apart. Just to the right of what was planned as the right hand side gap (GIN) the ditch right-angled backwards.

Lane 1 (GIN) – 1st Troop, 284th Assault Squadron

Bomb craters made the approach difficult, and an AVRE dropped out with clutch trouble. Then the lane commander, the Officer Commanding 284 Assault Squadron, realised that he was off line. He made a 'recce' on foot, found Team 2, with an AVRE in the ditch, roughly where he should be crossing. This meant that his team was entirely missing the ditch, which had turned back with a right angle, and was running parallel to it. Consequently he reconnoitred a crossing place and veered his team to its left to cross at as sharp an angle as possible. The snake was pushed over the ditch and was being made ready to fire when an enormous explosion knocked everyone flat. It was the RUM snake being fired. Soon the GIN snake was fired, knocking everyone in RUM down. The bridge was then dropped perfectly though, as with RUM, chespale was required to improve the approach, and then the Crabs crossed.

Lane 2 (RUM) – 2nd Troop, 16th Assault Squadron

Unfortunately the Bofors gun was firing 200 yards to the right, and the leading AVRE arrived just on the right angle and, not recognising its surrounding, fell in the AT ditch. The snake was then launched across the ditch and fired successfully, and the bridge was dropped, this being controlled by the crew commanders on foot.

The leading Crab, the direction keeper, could not mount the bridge as the ground was too soft so it was backed out and a sledge load of chespale bundles drawn up. These were laid on the approach to the bridge but were not enough so a fascine was dropped and broken up. The Crabs could then cross, but only with difficulty. An AVRE then crossed and dropped a fascine on the far side of the bridge for the same purpose. The AVREs then rallied back.

Lane 3 (ALE) – 3rd Troop, 16th Assault Squadron.

This team found itself off line and, correcting this arrived at the ditch at an angle. The snake broke so the opposite bank was petarded to detonate mines. The bridge was dropped and chespale laid as with the other lanes. The petarding could not have been as effective as a snake as one AVRE was lost on a mine.

The Crabs – 1st Lothian and Border Yeomanry.

On both GIN and RUM four out of the five Crabs went up on mines, the two survivors joined forces and made a single lane. On ALE all Crabs got through, but all were to be disabled on an unexpected minefield.

At first the Germans were not sure where the gaps were even though they must have seen the SBG bridges, and they searched the AT ditch with mortars. Presumably Strongpoint 8, where the most well placed observers would have been, was having its own troubles. But, once the moon came out the shelling and mortaring of the gaps started. This was well under way when the leading company of the 5th Cameronians crossed at 4.00am.

This company came under heavy fire and had several casualties, and suffered a *'temporary loss of orientation'*. Soon, though, the battalion advanced and captured Strongpoint 11 and cleared Fontaine-la-Mallet thereby providing an axis for wheeled vehicles for the subsequent advance into Le Havre.

Amusingly after the Cameronians had occupied Strongpoint 11 the German telephone rang, merely a routine call. The Company Commander answered the call and invited the German caller to surrender. The offer was refused but it was later found that several others had been plugged into the conversation and accepted the offer as soon as possible.

The German Collapse

On the 11th September progress was spectacular. The 49th Division captured the southern plateau, attacking from the north with 147th Brigade, supported by 7RTR and 107 RAC, though the latter also seems to have supported a 51st Division battalion, and from Harfleur in the east with 146th Brigade, supported by 9RTR. By nightfall they had reached Fort de Tourneville. The 51st Division, supported by two Yeomanry regiments, cleared the Foret de Montgeon up to Fort St Addresse.

The next day the German commander, Colonel Wildemuth, whose wife and children had recently been killed by the RAF in a raid on Berlin, surrendered. He had been wounded and surrendered in bed with his medals pinned on his pyjamas. He had been quite realistic about the battle and had told his troops to surrender rather than try to fight against tanks without appropriate weapons.

In conclusion it must be stated that, if the fall of Le Havre seems inevitable, the defence against the initial assault on the northern front was almost successful. If a few more mines had been deeply laid as they were in the middle gap, or if there had been a few more guns in concrete emplacements covering the minefield, it could have been that that attack would have failed. But it would have only delayed the inevitable.

To a certain extent the triumph was more apparent than real. The real objectives, the docks, were systematically destroyed by the Germans and would not be available for use until 9th October.

The assault of Le Havre marked an important step forwards in the progress of Infantry Tank Warfare. The specialized armour had now been deployed away from the Normandy beaches and the operation they had been primarily developed for, and were now accepted as an important part of a mechanised army. This had great implications for any AT defence depending on obstacles or mines. Also some use, even if rather limited, had been made of Kangaroos, and experience gathered to point the way forward for these new vehicles.

Operation Guildford

The assault of Blerick was that rare event, a military operation that went almost entirely to plan. The Germans were defending an old town, with narrow winding streets and many cellars, so it had to be captured by infantry, but because of the wire and mines a conventional infantry attack would have suffered heavy casualties and may not have succeeded. Instead the assault was a great success for specialised armour.

Blerick stands on the western bank of the Maas (Meuse), it is a suburb of Venlo which is on the eastern bank. The strategic aim of the Allies was to reduce all the German bridgeheads on the western side of the river, and Blerick was to be captured by 44th Brigade of 15th Scottish Division.

Blerick is situated in a slight concave curve of the river, the approach from the west is flat and open, it is overlooked by tall buildings in Blerick and Venlo, and by the high ground to the east of Venlo, so observation for German artillery would be good. The Germans were believed to have around 100 guns available to shell the attackers. *(See Sketch 5)*

The defences were based on an AT ditch dug from bank to bank fully enclosing Blerick from the west. It was over three miles long. In front and behind it were trenches and wire, and the main minefields were behind it. These were in the centre part of the front. The weak point of the defences was that the only bridge over the Maas to Venlo had been brought down, and the river was 150 yards wide, so the garrison could be neither reinforced nor withdrawn. The garrison was approximately a battalion.

An account of this action is given here in three parts. The first is a series of quotes from the manual 'The Characteristics and Tactical Employment of Specialised Armour' mentioned earlier in this chapter. Secondly is an account of the plan, and thirdly an account of what actually happened.

The Manual

' *PART IV – SPECIALISED ARMOUR IN THE ASSAULT* *INTRODUCTION*

Tactical Technique
1. This part deals with the employment of existing specialised armoured equipments in the assault on a strongly fortified inland position and in the beach assault. The technique described is as finally agreed between infantry formations and 79th Armoured Division. It is the result of experience gained during the campaign in North-West Europe and is, in principle, the technique successfully employed on several occasions, such as the attack on Blerick.

The Problem of the Assault.
2. The problem facing the infantry in an assault of this nature differs little from that of any other attack except that an artificial obstacle, or series of obstacles, have to be crossed before the objectives can be reached. Special equipment is therefore provided to make ways through and

across these obstacles to enable the infantry with their supporting arms and armour to reach their objectives.

Obstacles.
3. The main obstacles to be expected are:-
> *(a) Minefields – anti-tank, anti-personnel or mixed.*
> *(b) Anti-tank Ditches.*
> *(c) Wire.*
> *(d) Concrete walls and other concrete and metal obstacles.*

4. Minefields will almost invariably be present in any defensive layout and wire and anti-tank ditches will often be found in conjunction with them. These obstacles, either alone or in combination, are easily and quickly constructed and are more commonly met with than concrete obstructions which are generally to be found only in very highly organised defensive positions.

Equipment required.
5. The types of special equipment, some or all of which will be required in an assault of this nature, are:-
> *(a) Flails, to clear lanes through the minefields.*
> *(b) AVRE's, bridgelayers, Arks and tank dozers to bridge or breach anti-tank ditches and other obstacles and to reduce concrete defences and obstructions.*
> *(c) Flamethrowers, to assault with flame.*

6. Normal armoured equipment, such as gun tanks, to give close support and armoured personnel carriers to ensure a quick infantry follow-up, will also be required.

Phases.
7. The gapping of the minefield and other obstacles by specialised armour and the attack through these gaps by infantry is one operation, commanded, in the brigade assault, by the infantry brigade commander. The operation is, however, divided into two phases:-

(a) <u>Breaching Phase</u> – making the gaps by the Breaching Force, composed primarily of special armoured equipment.

(b) <u>Follow Up Phase</u> – The assault through the gaps by the Follow Up Force compose of infantry and their supporting arms.

Composition of the Breaching Team

21. One Breaching Team is required for each lane. Its composition and the nature of the devices carried by the AVRE's will depend on the problem presented by the enemy defences. Where there is a minefield in combination with an anti-tank ditch a typical Breaching Team would be:-

Lane Commander (in an AVRE)

Flail troop.

AVRE bridge, or ARK, or Tank Bridgelayer.

AVRE fascine (in reserve in case of failure of the bridge).

Spare AVRE, if available (probably also with fascine, to deal with unexpected obstacles such as road craters).

Armoured Personnel Carrier carrying:-

Lane Marking Party (until a satisfactory mechanical method has been produced).

A small RE party to carry out a final check for mines, if necessary.

Infantry Component.

51. This should be positioned where it can quickly be called forward to assist the flails or to establish the "Breach Head" immediately the lanes are through. The infantry should not follow behind the flails during the gapping operation or they will suffer heavy casualties from enemy artillery and mortar fire, and, possibly from exploding mines.........They might, on occasions, be held in armoured personnel carriers in the Forming Up Place.

<u>*Action of the Breaching Team.*</u>

56. (d)....the detailed procedure is as follows:-

 i. *Flails sweep up to the ditch.*

 ii. *Flails reverse until they can sweep a path to either or both sides of the breach wide enough to take AVRE's*

 iii. *AVRE's sent forward by Lane Commander who moves up himself.*

 iv. *AVRE's bridge anti-tank ditch.*

 v. *AVRE's reverse clear of ditch.*

 vi. *Flails rejoin swept path, cross ditch and continue flailing until far edge of minefield is reached.*

 vii. *AVRE's turn off into "parking ground" swept by flails.*

 viii. *Flails take up fire positions, hull-down if possible, on the far side of minefield to support infantry assault until relieved by gun tanks.*

<u>*Use of armoured personnel carriers for Follow Up Force*</u>

65. The use of armoured personnel carriers enables the infantry of the Follow Up Force to be brought to the assault straight from the Assembly Area or from even further back. They can have a hot meal before embussing, arrive fresh for the battle and are saved casualties near the Forming Up Place and Start Line, which, in an operation of this nature, are always likely to be under heavy enemy mortar and artillery fire.

66. Whether armoured personnel carriers are used to carry the infantry through the lanes or whether they dismount before reaching the minefield will depend on the proximity of their objectives to the obstacle. If the enemy defences are close to the minefield....there will not usually be sufficient advantage to be gained from taking the armoured personnel carriers into the lanes to compensate for the risk of blocking the gaps at a critical stage in the operation. If,

146

however, rapid exploitation to more distant objectives by the Follow Up Force is planned, and there is no serious risk of casualties to the armoured personnel carriers in the lanes from anti-tank guns or mines, it will be advisable for infantry to remain mounted.'

The Plan
The assault was to be carried out by the 44th Brigade: Brigadier Cumming-Bruce
    8th Royal Scots
    6th Royal Scots Fusiliers
    6th Kings Own Scottish Borderers
    7th Seaforth Highlanders, from 46th Brigade

The attackers had the support of 31st Tank Brigade Group: Brigadier Knight
    107th Regiment RAC, two squadrons (Churchills)
    22nd Dragoons (Crabs)
    81st Assault Regt RE, one squadron (SBG Bridges)
    49th Armoured Personnel Carrier Regt (Kangaroos)
    Fife & Forfar Yeomanry, one squadron (Crocodiles)

The artillery support, which was provided by three Army Groups Royal Artillery, totalled 400 guns including super-heavies, also there was the 1st Canadian Rocket Projector Unit equipped with six 'mattresses'. This was the first time these weapons had been used in war. Each 'mattress' could fire 350 rockets simultaneously.

The assault was broken down into two phases: the armoured phase, and the infantry phase.

The armoured phase was dominated by the Breaching Force. This was broken down into two Assault Teams, the northern one was to consist of the three troops of Crabs of 'A' sqn, and one from 'B' sqn, 22nd Dragoons, and half the

Assault sqn, being four SBG Bridges and two AVREs with fascines. The southern Assault Team was similar, but based on 'C' sqn, 22nd Dragoons. Each Assault Team was supported by a squadron of tanks.

Each Assault Team was responsible for three lanes, so each gapping team was one troop of Crabs and an SBG Bridge, each Assault Team had a troop of Crabs, an SBG Bridge and two fascines in reserve. The 22nd Dragoons had a troop of Crabs in reserve.

The Breaching Force was to advance behind a barrage and smokescreen, the barrage moved at 100 yards every two minutes. First would come gun tanks which would take up positions to provide fire support. The Crabs would flail six lanes up to the AT ditch, these were numbered 1 to 6, north to south. After the Crabs would come the SBG bridges, one for each lane. The Crabs would cross the bridges and continue flailing up to the outskirts of town. That would conclude the armoured phase. As can be seen it was just a refinement of the methods used at Le Havre except that it was to be carried out in daylight.

The infantry stage showed the greatest innovation. The first two battalions to advance were to be waiting in their Kangaroos, the 49th APCR consisted of two squadrons each of a nominal strength of 53 Kangaroos and capable of lifting a battalion. The objectives of these battalions were in the centre of Blerick. The Kangaroos would then return, load up the next two battalions, the second flight, and take them to their objectives in the northern and southern parts of town.

There was a deception plan laid on over the two nights before the assault. Tank noises were broadcast, and showy patrol activity was staged which, among other things, involved making gaps in the wire. The assaulting troops were kept as far back from the start line as possible, but the second flight battalions had to move forward to speed up the Kangaroos' turn-round time.

The Assault
The major problem made itself felt on 2nd December, when it rained. At 2.0 pm the ground was so soft that Brigadier Knight began to doubt that the operation was possible, but at 9.0 pm the rain stopped and he changed his mind. At 4.0 am next morning the corps commander gave the go-ahead.

The battle started with the barrage at 5.25 am, on 3rd December 1944. The division's history states that never before had so many guns, over 400, concentrated on such a small area.

Before they reached the start line a troop of five Crabs of the northern Assault Team bogged down so badly that they had to be replaced by the spare 'B' sqn troop. The others stayed on the roads as much as possible. In the Assault Team one Crab was blown up on a mine before reaching the start line. It was common German practice to lay a few mines in front of a minefield to confuse the attackers as to where the front edge of it was. A small number of the Churchill gun tanks also stuck and had to be dragged out.

At 7.45 the Breaching Force crossed the start line. Progress was slow but definite. On the right one of the leading Crabs was knocked out by a panzerfaust which killed the commander and wounded two of the crew, which shows that regardless of how heavy the artillery bombardment is, there will always be some surviving defenders ready to fight back. Crabs, of course, cannot fire their main armament while flailing, so this resistance was handled with MGs and grenades. Two lanes, 5 and 6, were through to the ditch with bridge laid, by 9.15am.

On the left the mud was even worse and lane 3 had to be abandoned, but lanes 1 and 2 were cleared up to the ditch, with a bridge laid by 9.0am. As soon as the bridges were laid Brigadier Cumming-Bruce ordered the first flight of Kangaroos forward. The southern battalion, the Royal Scots, drove into Blerick to debus, but the northern battalion, the Royal Scots Fusiliers, seeing how muddy the ground was and that they were not being shelled, proceeded on foot because it was thought that the Kangaroos might bog down and that would hold up the second flight. This left the Crabs on the left two lanes standing vulnerably at the eastern edge of the minefield, and firing into Blerick, for around an hour, but fortunately suffering no casualties. The RSF were later on their objective than were the RS, but both had gone firm by 1.0 pm. The second flight followed according to plan except that the northern battalion, the Seaforths, was 90 minutes late due to the mud.

While the Crabs on the right were withdrawing they were caught in mortar fire that killed one commander. Some of the Crabs became bogged down and had to be temporally abandoned but by 3.0 pm the battle was over, for a total cost of 50 casualties.

The immediate impression produced by this battle is one of the huge resources required to subdue one battalion, but really these resources, artillery and armour, were there to overcome the defences, not the garrison. Once the assaulting infantry were in Blerick it was, as a gross simplification, four battalions against one, odds that would have been by no means excessive in the American Civil War. The defensive power of modern weapons was there for all to see.

Comments

Specialised armour came into existence as a part of predictable tactical development. Infantry tanks were there to help the infantry forward against the anti-infantry defensive weapons, MGs and wire, that had proven so successful in the Great War, but they could not cope with minefields. Mine warfare was the most significant tactical development of the Second World War, and it is not surprising that special equipment had to be designed to counter it. Fortunately a good deal of the development work had been done during the Great War and flail tanks soon made an appearance.

Flails were the most important special armoured vehicle, but as has been shown, far from the only ones. Bridges and AVREs were required to help the flails and Infantry tanks forward, and Crocodiles overcame positions that the infantry could not reach. The basic task of specialised armour was an extension of that of Infantry tanks, to support the infantry in the assault.

Unfortunately there was never enough specialised armour and it did not have time before the end of the war to make its capabilities known to the armoured divisions. However because of the success of the armoured divisions in the pursuit stage this omission was probably not that important except in one case. It has already been suggested that if the Guards Armoured Division in September 1944 had a few bridging tanks it might have got to Arnhem in time.

Chapter 8: Kangaroos

During the Normandy campaign high infantry casualties resulted in the requirement being formulated for an armoured vehicle to carry the infantry forward so that they would arrive on their objective at the same time as their supporting tanks without enduring the casualties and fatigue that had hitherto been their lot.

On 31st July Lieutenant General Simonds, the commander of 2nd Canadian Corps, negotiated from the Americans an extension of the loan from them of three regiments worth of Priest self-propelled 105-mm guns, a total of 72 guns. He also got permission to temporally modify them to turn them into armoured personnel carriers.

The modifications consisted mainly of removing the 105-mm and blocking up the now unnecessary embrasure with ad-hoc armour. Various sources were tried for this ad-hoc armour, finally mild steel plate from a Caen rolling mill was used, presumably for ease of cutting and welding. Two plates were used, the gap between them being filled with sand.

This work was done by a Canadian Advanced Workshop Detachment codenamed 'Kangaroo'. This word was applied to the converted AFVs.

Each Kangaroo could easily carry, apart from its driver, 10 infantrymen and their weapons, and if necessary a good number more. The Kangaroos were operated by an *ad-hoc* Canadian unit. Some of the Kangaroos retained their .5-inch MG, and over half had a No 19 wireless set.

Work converting the Priests started on 2nd August 1944 and was finished late on the 5th. Late on the 7th August these vehicles jumped off on Operation Totalize. This was an amazing triumph of improvisation. Operation Totalize was a success as was the part the Kangaroos played in it. It was quickly followed by Operation Tractable. Later the Kangaroos took part in the assault of Le Havre and some other operations before they had to be re-converted to Priests and handed back to the Americans.

The result of this experience was the formation of two regiments of Kangaroos, one Canadian, 1st Canadian Armoured Carrier Regiment, and one British, 49th Armoured Personnel Carrier Regiment which started life as 49th RTR. The Kangaroos were now converted Rams, these were Canadian tanks, but soon other tanks were used.

The work converting Priests and tanks to Kangaroos was all carried out on a commonsense *ad-hoc* basis, and it was not until 1949, with the publication of the manual 'Tactical Handling of TANKS in co-operation with INFANTRY', that there was an official statement defining their characteristics:

Section 3 - THE CHARACTERISTICS OF ARMOURED PERSONNEL CARRIERS

1. *The armoured personnel carrier (APC) of an Armoured Transport Regiment RAC is of similar design to a tank but is lighter and has, in consequence, a better cross country performance, since it has no turret and no primary armament. It is not, however, an armoured fighting vehicle but is designed for troop-carrying purposes only with the object of giving armoured mobility to the infantry thus enabling them to arrive quickly at the vital point of the battlefield, fresh and with the minimum of casualties. Each APC is equipped with the current wireless set in use with the equivalent type of tank, whilst the vehicles of regimental, squadron,*

and troop headquarters each carry two sets. Apart from being turretless and mounting only one light automatic of limited frontal traverse, the APC is, therefore, identical to a tank and can be used in any phase of battle where tanks can manoeuvre. It is, however, equally vulnerable to AP shot and to mines, whilst the infantry being carried are more susceptible to HE shell than are the crew of a tank when the turret is closed down.

2. *The roles of the APC may be summarised as follows:-*
    (a) *Advance to contact.- To carry a proportion of the leading infantry, thus giving added speed to the advance.*
    (b) *Attack.- To carry the infantry on to, or close to, their objective.*
    (c) *Pursuit.- To carry the infantry moving in support of the leading armour.*
    (d) *Defence.- To carry the infantry in a deliberate counter-attack in conjunction with tanks.*
    (e) *Withdrawal.- To carry the rearmost infantry in order to confer the necessary mobility which will enable them to make a clean break from contact with the enemy.*

Kangaroo Tactics

Because of the small number of Kangaroos and the lateness of the stage of the war in which they were issued, tactics for their use were not standardised during the war, and no manuals on this subject were issued. There was no better statement of the principles of their employment than that in Lieutenant General Simond's appreciation for Operation Totalize when he wrote:

'The essentials are that the infantry shall be carried in bullet and splinter-proof vehicles to their actual objectives.'

The concept was not immediately popular with many senior officers who observed that a Kangaroo was a large AFV transporting only a small number of infantry and taking up a lot of space on the road, but experience was to show that a small number of soldiers on the objective could be more useful than a large number still trying to get there.

Regardless of what senior officers thought, Kangaroos proved very popular with fighting soldiers. In the book 'The Story of 79th Armoured Division' a Canadian officer is quoted as saying *'since the substitution of the musket for the cross-bow, there has been no development in infantry equipment comparable to the arrival of the Kangaroo'.* However in north-western Europe tactics for the use of Kangaroos developed slowly. The problem was that the Kangaroo regiments were switched frequently from one division to another, and they were usually regarded as little more than armoured lorries by the units they were transporting. However their potential was there for all to see, particularly as they now had a crew of two and carried one or two MGs. So gradually they started to work in close co-operation with tanks on the battlefield. The war ended before tactics were standardised and, as can be seen, two regiments for both the Canadian and British armies were not going to cause a military revolution.

As will be seen, surprisingly more imaginative use of Kangaroos was made in Italy.

After the war there were limited trials with the conversion of other tanks to Kangaroos but the concept was not really pursued and the Kangaroo tactics section of the 1949 manual mentioned in the previous section may be taken as being a statement of the most advanced thinking about APCs at the end of the war:

Section 19 – THE USE OF ARMOURED PERSONNEL CARRIERS

2. *The most dangerous moment for the infantry is when they are dismounting from their APCs. At the same time, the most dangerous time for dismounted infantry is the last 200 yards of the attack. No two sets of conditions are the same, and nice judgement will be required to decide when to dismount the infantry. It is clearly desirable to avoid the infantry bearing the brunt of both these periods of greatest danger, and one of them can be largely eliminated by driving to the objective. The nature of the ground and the enemy's dispositions may sometimes give rise, however, to a need for dismounting short of the objective. To expose loaded APCs to well-aimed anti-tank fire may, however, well cause higher infantry casualties and a loss of APCs which would prejudice the success of further phases of the battle. Nevertheless, in spite of all the difficulties named, the role of the APC in the attack is to carry the assaulting infantry on to, or as near as possible to, their objective, fresh and fighting fit. The demoralizing effect on the enemy of the sudden arrival of the infantry, mounted in APCs and covered by tanks, in their midst over-rides all other considerations.*

3. *APCs cannot support each other forward in the same way as tanks. To carry out their role successfully and to minimize casualties to both infantry and vehicles, a sound co-ordination of artillery and tank support is, therefore, essential*

during the final stages of the advance in order to assist the APCs on to the objective.

4. *As APCs will normally operate in conjunction with tanks, their handling and movement will depend on the action of the tanks. Tanks may lead in order to cover the advance of the APCs, in which case the latter will conform to the speed of the tanks. Alternatively, the tanks may operate on one or both flanks. Tanks will support infantry in APCs in the same way as they support infantry on their feet, that is, by moving by bounds from fire position to fire position according to the ground. Against defence in depth, it will be unusual for tanks to be able to break in without some dismounted infantry assistance. Nevertheless, in an attack to a definite and limited objective it may be possible for a proportion of the infantry reorganisation force to drive steadily from the start line to the dismounting place.*

5. *Keeping direction is one of the most difficult tasks in an operation of this nature, particularly at night or just before dusk and dawn. Searchlights, light anti-aircraft guns firing tracer, check lines or any other means of assisting keeping direction, should be used. In the haze and heat of the battle, it is very difficult for infantry when they dismount from the APCs to discover their whereabouts in relation to their objective and to each other, and during a move in APCs the infantry must constantly look out and keep their bearings. Commanders at all levels must be well forward so that they can see and control the battlefield and be in a position to deal with the unexpected.*

Chapter 9: Kangaroos in Action

Kangaroos first came into existence for Operation Totalize, which carried over into Operation Tractable, but it was always realised that the Priest Kangaroos would have to be returned to the Americans. Consequently if the Kangaroo concept was to be carried further other vehicles would have to be converted, and a stronger organisation set up for a unit to operate them.

Both these requirements were met by the Canadians, who set up the 1st Canadian Armoured Personnel Carrier Squadron – this would soon become a regiment – and started converting Ram tanks.

The Ram was the Canadian Cruiser. It was a good tank but its turret was too small to mount a 75-mm in comfort and its production was halted in favour of the Sherman. But the production was not wasted and the Ram hulls were put to a number of uses, Kangaroos being but one. The Ram was lighter than the Priest and the other tanks in service; the Churchill, Cromwell and Sherman. It was also smaller and could carry no more than an infantry section, ten men if at full strength.

The Canadian Ram unit was the only such unit until December. Up till then, during the great pursuit through France and Belgium, there had seemed little point in creating another, but once the fighting had bogged down, literally, this view changed. 49 RTR was converted to a Kangaroo regiment and renamed 49th Armoured Personnel Carrier Regiment. At roughly the same time the Canadian regiment dropped the word 'Personnel' from its title. These seemingly pointless changes to regimental names may hint at a deeper meaning. The Canadians were keen to present the Kangaroos at fighting vehicles, not just busses, whereas the British change hints at down-grading from 'Tanks'.

Both the British and the Canadian regiments became a part of the 79th Armoured Division. These new regiments were organised as two squadrons of 53 Kangaroos each so, equating a Kangaroo to an infantry section each regiment could carry two battalions. Demand for Kangaroos became so great that a further squadron was added to the APC Regiment in March 1945.

The creation of the British regiment was in time for the assault of Blerick. After this, up to the end of the war in North-Western Europe, the British regiment was employed in transporting troops of six infantry divisions, one airborne division, an armoured brigade and an armoured division. With switching around like this it is not surprising that tactics for Kangaroos developed slowly. The infantry divisions regarded them merely as armoured lorries, and the occasional attempt to use them more imaginatively could result in disaster.

One such disaster occurred to the east of Cleve during the Reichswald fighting on 12th February 1945. Some Kangaroos had been transporting a battalion of Seaforth Highlanders, after the troops had debussed the Kangaroos were ordered to advance in front of them. They drove into the field of fire of a self-propelled gun and several were knocked out (see note).

Even worse, on 30th March, a Kangaroo squadron working with 53rd Division ran into an AT screen and lost eight Kangaroos. But these cases were exceptions, in general the Kangaroos speeded up infantry operations and increased flexibility. The bulk of the Kangaroos were with infantry divisions, but of greater interest were those operations carried out in the last weeks of the war in support of armoured formations.

On 28th March one squadron of Kangaroos was supporting 7th Armoured Division. Following a hard fight at Stadtlohn the Kangaroos and 1RTR staged a six mile breakthrough to Heek. On 1st April they covered 20 miles to Metelen. The infantry, 1/5th Queens, found the Kangaroos dirty, noisy and uncomfortable for long journeys, but safer. After the fighting at Ibbenburen even these distances seemed short, but by then the division was coming across only negligible resistance. However even though it was in an armoured division the Kangaroo-borne infantry was not used in direct cooperation with the tanks but was transported forward for infantry fighting. Similarly the 4th Somerset Light Infantry, in Canadian Kangaroos, came under the command of 8th Armoured Brigade for one day, 30th March, but that was to take part in the break-out battle, the tanks swanned through without them.

Possibly the most interesting use of Kangaroos was made by 4th Armoured Brigade, which is not surprising since it was commanded by Brigadier Carver, the youngest brigadier in the army and the future field marshal. The brigade had lost an armoured regiment, detached to support an infantry division, but had under command a battalion in Kangaroos and its motor battalion in half-tracks, so it was formed into two tank/infantry battle groups.

In this formation, starting from Rethem on 14th April 1945, it was able to stage a series of outflanking manoeuvres, squadron/company groups leapfrogging past each other. The Germans of 2nd Marine Division fought hard but had no answer to this type of attack.

It must not be forgotten that mechanised formations consume vast quantities of fuel and ammunition, so any advance by one should not be so deep as to present a long and vulnerable flank to enemy counter-attacks which could cut off supplies. Considering this, perhaps the best employment of tank/infantry battle groups is a series of break-throughs, as is illustrated by the 78th Division in the Argenta Gap battle.

As can be seen the British army did not fully exploit the potential of the Kangaroo, which was a pity.

Note:
This action is a little difficult to understand, even the number of Kangaroos knocked out varies sharply between various accounts, the number of vehicle casualties and sources of information being:
Three, 'Through Mud and Blood', B Perret, London, 1975
Four, '6th Guards Tank Brigade', P Forbes, London, no date and The Battalion War Diary, TNA WO171/5270
Seven, 'The Story of the 79th Armoured Division', July 1945.

Operation Totalize
The First use of Kangaroos

By the end of July 1944 the German army in Normandy was starting to show signs of weakness and General Montgomery instructed the G.O.C.-in-C. 1st Canadian Army to prepare a plan for an offensive in the Falaise direction.

The German front was close to where it was at the end of Operation Goodwood. The advanced line *(Vorgeschobene Stellung)* ran along Verrieres ridge, generally rising to Point 122. The defences were centred on villages and the ground was open enough for the German AT guns to take full advantage of their range, but verdant and close enough for these guns to be easily camouflaged.

The main line of resistance *(Hauptkampflinie)*, actually, like the advanced line a deep defensive zone, was around five miles to the rear, far enough back so that the artillery supporting an attack on the first line would have to be moved forward to attack the second.

The action was to be carried out by 2nd Canadian Corps. Its commander, Lieutenant General Simonds produced an appreciation on 1st August which outlined how the offensive would be carried out. The appreciation described a three phase operation:

Phase 1, Two infantry divisions, each supported by an armoured brigade, were to capture the high ground towards the rear of the German front line positions, mop up bypassed German troops and secure the flanks.

Phase 2, An armoured division and an infantry division were to break into the German second line.

Phase 3, A fresh armoured division would pursue in the direction of Falaise.

When General Simonds drew up the appreciation, both lines were held by troops of the 1st SS-PanzerKorps, but before the operation started they were replaced by a fairly ordinary infantry division. The Canadian command assumed that the SS divisions were to be deployed for a defence-in-depth, so Phase 2 of the offensive would be that much more difficult.

The problem facing the Canadians was how to keep the advance moving. All previous offensives had ground to a halt once the advancing troops had moved out of the range of their supporting artillery, so plainly something new had to be tried. The answer was twofold:

Phase 1 would be carried out at night, with the infantry being carried forward in Kangaroos.

Phase 2 would be prepared by a heavy bomber raid.

The day before he produced his appreciation, General Simonds had ordered the conversion of 72 Priest self-propelled guns into Kangaroos. They were sometimes called 'unfrocked priests' or even 'holy rollers'. The idea might have sprung fully formed from the General's brain, but as General O'Connor had identified the need for such vehicles before Operation Goodwood, it is more likely that the requirement was well known, Simonds just had the opportunity.

The operation, codenamed 'Totalize', was originally planned to start late on 8th August, but it was moved forward 24 hours after a request from Montgomery. This meant that some of the infantry units only received their Kangaroos a few hours before jumping off, but with the very limited role the Kangaroos were to undertake, that was probably not very important.

The 2nd Canadian Corps originally consisted of the 2nd and 3rd Infantry Divisions, the 4th Armoured Division and the 2nd Armoured Brigade, it was reinforced for Operation Totalize with 51st (Highland) Infantry Division and the Polish Armoured Division, and two British armoured brigades.

Phase 1 of the battle was to be undertaken by two infantry divisions, 51st Highland Division to the east, and 2nd Canadian Infantry Division to the west. The Kangaroos were to be split equally between them. In both cases by adding all their Bren Gun carriers and half-tracks to the 36 Kangaroos allocated to them they could provide an infantry brigade with cross-country transport.

Because of the problems with maintaining direction and keeping together it was General Simonds' decision that each mounted battalion would advance in a closed-up column four vehicles wide. This was essential to get through any flailed gap in a minefield and to facilitate quick deployment on foot when the troops dismounted. The essential aid to direction keeping was Bofors guns firing tracer rounds over the columns. A direction finding radio device had been developed but, mostly because of the lie of the land, most units could not make it work. Also some tanks had compasses mounted, but most of these soon lost their accuracy.

The initial objectives of the 51st Highland Division were Cramesnil, St Aignan-de-Cramesnil, Garcelles-Secqueville and Lorguichon Wood. The secondary objectives were Secqueville-la-Campagne and the woods to its east and south. These objectives would require four battalions, but there was only enough transport for three, the fourth must go on foot. The first three objectives were allocated to 154th Brigade, which was to be supported by the tanks of 33rd Armoured Brigade. Lorguichon was to be taken by a battalion of 152nd Brigade.

The divisional commander decided that the four battalions with their various supports would advance on two axes. The western column, aimed at Garcelles-Secqueville was to consist of two mounted battalions in tandem and the eastern column of one. Each column was based on a carrier borne battalion following two squadrons of tanks and a squadron of Crabs, and followed by a further column of tanks, all in fours.

The principle was that the armoured commander was in overall command during the move, but once the troops had dismounted, the infantry commander took over.

On the western side of the break-in the initial objectives of 2nd Canadian Infantry Division were the area of Caillouet to Point 122, which was just to the west of Cramesnil, and the western flank, an area including May-sur-Orne and Fontenay-le-Marmion. The secondary objective was Bretteville-sur-Laize.

As with 51st Highland Division there were really four battalion sized objectives and transport was only available for three. Consequently the divisional commander, Major

General Foulkes decided to send the division's reconnaissance regiment to capture Point 122. This armoured car and carrier regiment included an infantry company and could be expected to hold a small objective for a short time. The other objectives were given to 4th Brigade, escorted by 2nd Canadian Armoured Brigade which had one regiment detached. The whole task force, which was termed 2nd Canadian Armoured Brigade group, was commanded by the armoured brigade commander, Brigadier Wyman. His approach was basically different to that of the Highland Division.

The armoured brigade group was divided into four forces, each with its own commander. It was to advance along two axes, the left being based on the reconnaissance regiment, the right on the infantry brigade. In front of each battalion sized column went units of the 'gapping force'. Each of these units was to consist of two troops of Shermans, two troops of Crabs and a troop of AVREs. They were to be led by the navigating officer.

The gapping force preceding the infantry brigade came under one commander, the three battalions plus ancillary units such as AT guns constituted the 'assault force' and came under the brigade commander. The left hand, eastern, column consisting of the reconnaissance regiment and gapping unit with AT guns all came under the reconnaissance regiment commander. The remaining tanks followed behind the four columns as a reserve, they were the 'fortress force'.

The organisation for the 2nd Canadian Armoured Brigade Group could well have been a good one had there been more time for training and rehearsals, but as the date of the operation had been moved forward a day, and units and equipment were still arriving only hours before jumping off, this time was not available. The gapping teams were only able to start rehearsals the evening before the operation started. The procedure for clearing any minefield encountered was to be slightly different from the standard one. A gap wide enough for four vehicles to drive through side by side was required. A normal gap was 24 feet wide but for this operation the gap would have to be 48 feet, so six flailing Crabs were needed, working in a lopsided 'V' formation.

The narrowness of the gaps being flailed meant that the battalion columns must keep in very close order. The three columns of the assault force covered a total front of 150 yards. This left only 50 yards between columns. All this was not made easier by the assault force following about five minutes behind the gapping force.

The AFV columns of the two mobile brigades formed up well behind the lines to ensure that they were not seen by the Germans. They moved forward so that they crossed the start line at 11.30 pm 7th August 1944. The bombing of the German positions on the flanks of the attack, that is on the west St Martin-de-Fontenay to Fontenay-le-Marmion, and on the east La Hogue to Garcelles-Secqueville, had started at 11.00 pm and ended at 11.40. Although these targets were marked by flare shells fired by the artillery of the attacking divisions the bombing was only partly successful, but 3,456 tons of bombs were dropped and the shock must have been stunning.

After crossing the start line the two brigades had to cover a mile to form up behind the first line of the barrage which began at 11.45. Difficulties immediately made themselves felt. The radio direction finding system worked for very few units, it was hopeless for most. Vehicle-borne compasses were thrown out by the barrage, and the clouds of dust thrown up by the bombing and the barrage made the trace rounds impossible to see and rendered ineffective attempts to generate some 'Monty's moonlight'. And, of course, the Germans were firing back.

The left hand column of 154th Brigade was 1st Black Watch and 1st Northamptonshire Yeomanry. As they struggled forward behind the barrage, which was advancing at one and a half miles per hour, things started to go wrong. Close to Bourguebus were two sunken lanes, obstacles to half-tracks, which bulldozers had made crossings over. These crossings were hard to find in the dark, then the Crabs found negotiating them difficult, this started to break up the column. The column was fortunate to just miss two minefields, but it ran into some German self-propelled guns which knocked out three Shermans, the flames of one lighting up the area. That was the only major mishap to this column which arrived on time close to Garcelles-Secqueville. Because of the general uncertainty about the Germans the infantry commander decided to keep his men mounted a little longer and they drove to just north of St Aignan-de-Cramesnil, where they dismounted and, after a 45 minutes wait while straggling Kangaroos and carriers caught up, cleared the village with covering fire from the tanks. They were then on their objective.

The right hand force consisted of two battalion/regimental columns. The leading column, 144 RAC and 7th Argyll and Sutherland Highlanders, soon dissolved into chaos. The leading three tanks, Honeys, carrying the navigating officer and two assistant navigators fell into bomb craters and from then on in the very limited visibility the vehicles seem to have struggled on almost individually in approximately the right direction. They were helped in this by the main road on their right, even though some vehicles got mixed up with the Canadian left hand column. Worse they actually fired on the Scottish left hand column, but with only MG fire that caused no casualties. The tricky part came when crossing the railway, only one vehicle at a time could do this and two tanks were knocked out here by panzerfausts.

Fortunately by 3.30am visibility improved, the barrage had ended and the moon had come out. The head of the column approached Cramesnil, the objective. One of the first tanks there was knocked out by a panzerfaust so the tank colonel decided that it was time for the infantry to dismount. This they did and after a wait to assemble the companies the village was secured by 7.0am.

The following column, 148 RAC and 7th Black Watch, had no trouble. It followed the leading column in near perfect order and by 5.30 had secured Garcelles-Secqueville.

The mounted advance of 154th Brigade had, overall, been a considerable success though, it must be noted that the marching troops had considerable difficulty and casualties in capturing their objectives. Being by-passed did not mean that German morale would crumble and though the Germans here were certainly not elite troops, they still put up a creditable fight. The chaos that the leading right hand column fell into meant that the Crabs could not have been used as they depended on rigid control. Fortunately this did not matter. The Canadians were not so lucky.

The left hand Canadian column, based on the Reconnaissance Regiment, started off following its Crabs through a minefield, from then on visibility, as elsewhere, was so bad that the column bumbled on south and finally settled close to Rocquancourt, thinking it was closer to its objective, Point 122, than it actually was.

The right hand Canadian force was remarkably successful despite what must have seemed at the time to be total chaos. The assault force was three battalion columns moving in parallel. They were, from east to west, the Royal Regiment of Canada, the Royal Hamilton Light Infantry and the Essex Scottish. The operation started according to plan but quite soon fire from the right flank caused both assault force and gapping force to veer slightly to the left. This resulted in the link between the assault force and the gapping force being broken, and the left hand gapping unit and infantry column passing Rocquancourt to the west. The central infantry column hit the village head on and actually drove right through it while the remainder went to the west as planned.

Once past Rocquancourt an increase in German fire halted the columns. This fire came from some SS troops retained in position when the rest of the SS corps was withdrawn. As the columns had been so scattered, the dismounted companies were in no state to continue the assault on foot.

The defenders had fought back well, and in the morning it was found that 14 half-tracks and two tank destroyers were missing, though no doubt some might have returned later. The chaos the attackers were in was only sorted out in the morning when the objectives were secured, and the fortress force came up to prepare to repel any counter-attack.

This concluded the use of Kangaroos in Operation Totalize. Despite what it might have looked like to those taking part, the use of Kangaroos had been a great success. After the Kangaroos were withdrawn the operation bogged down.

Operation Cygnet

Although Kangaroos were first used in North West Europe it is remarkable that the greatest enthusiasm for them and the greatest imagination in the way they were used was shown in Italy. General McCreery was very impressed by the reports he had heard of their use in France and he ordered the REME workshops to start converting Shermans and Priests. Enough Kangaroos were to have been supplied from the UK but never were and all those used by the 8th Army were locally produced. The Official History lists four anticipated advantages from their use: protection while on the move; better communications, especially with gun tanks;

carrying capacity for ammunition and personal kit; and a general morale boost that the lot of the infantry was being improved.

As they were produced the Kangaroos were issued to 9th Armoured Brigade because this brigade was responsible for operating the Landing Vehicles Tracked (LVTs) and DD tanks. The brigade gave them to the 4th Hussars.

The first use of Kangaroos was to be in Operation Cygnet, in which elements of 56th Division were to clear a salient jutting to the east of the River Senio. This salient was roughly parallelogram shaped, being bounded on the north and the west sides by the Senio, and on the east by the Canal Naviglio. The long axis, northeast to south-west, was about five miles long, and the short axis about three. The basis of the plan was that three squadrons of Shermans, supported by infantry in Kangaroos, were to sweep through the salient, starting at the south face and finishing up by capturing the bridge close to San Severo.

The leading echelon of tanks was to consist of two squadrons from 2RTR and one from 10th Hussars. The infantry battalion was the 2nd/6th Queens, carried in 53 Kangaroos of 'C' squadron, 4th Hussars.

The action took place of 4th January 1945, it was all a little rushed in order to take advantage of the frost. There was to be a mounted infantry company following each of the three tank squadrons, and an extra one securing the start line with a further tank squadron.

'C' squadron secured the start line at first light, 7.15 am, progress being slow due to mist and coloured smoke. There was a shortage of artillery ammunition so there would be a greater than usual reliance on aerial support, so for this, coloured smoke was fired to act as a bomb line.

The three squadrons, sweeping northwards, met only sporadic resistance, the infantry was mostly employed in 'mopping up' by-passed Germans. However by mid afternoon aircraft had reported that some German tanks might be moving up on the west of the Senio to cross the bridge by San Severo. To prevent this it was necessary to capture the strongpoint of Villa Bulzacca. A mounted company, escorted by some 'C' squadron tanks, was rushed up for the task. A short artillery bombardment was organised then, just as the sun was starting to set, at 4.35 pm, 'A' squadron came up to within 200 yards of the villa and poured 75-mm HE into it for several minutes, then they moved forward to 100 yards and hosed it with Browning MGs. Then the Kangaroos surged forward through the line of tanks, drove right up to the buildings where the troops dismounted and captured them without casualties, a scene worthy of panzer-grenadiers at their best. That, apart from the mopping up, concluded the operation.

This operation was itself not that important, but it was the first use of Kangaroos in Italy, so the lessons drawn from it were important:
   a) Kangaroos should be escorted by tanks, raising the question should Kangaroo units have organic tanks.
   b) Kangaroos should follow directly behind tanks to take advantage of the enemy's disorganisation.
   c) It may be better for infantry involved in mopping up to be under infantry command, whereas those directly cooperating with tanks must be under armour command.

Operation Buckland,
The 78th Division at the Argenta Gap

By spring 1945 the war was drawing to a close, and German forces were in retreat both on the eastern and western fronts. However in Italy they were standing firm.

Italy is a long, thin country with a mountainous spine from which a series of rivers runs, both east and west, to the sea. The Germans manned a succession of defence lines, based on these rivers. These were overcome, one after the other, but the garrisons just withdrew to the next and the substantial allied armoured forces managed little more than a hesitant follow-up. In April 1945 plans were made to improve upon this. The Germans were holding positions very roughly 30 miles to the south of the major river Po. The aim was to destroy these forces before they could withdraw across the river, not just to force them back across it.

The offensive, codenamed 'Operation Grapeshot', was to be undertaken by both the American and British armies and the British part of the operation was called 'Operation Buckland'. The British 8th Army was on the eastern side where there were three potential British thrust lines and the army commander chose the Via Adriatica. There were several reasons for this decision, but the most important was that when compared to other routes the general trend of north running roads and comparative lack of water obstacles made exploitation by this route the easiest. These roads, of course, would also make it easy for the Germans to bring up reinforcements. Unfortunately the first few miles of any advance up the Via Adriatica ran through the Argenta Gap. The task of forcing the Gap was given to General Keightley, the commander of 5th Corps. *(See Sketches 6 and 7)*

General Keightley broke down the task of 5th Corps into three phases:

i.   8th Indian and 2nd New Zealand Divisions to cross the Senio,

ii.   The same divisions to cross the Santerno, five mile behind the Senio,

iii. 78th and 56th Divisions to break out through the Argenta Gap.

The Argenta Gap was the strip of land around the Via Adriatica. It ran with Lake Comacchio and the related inundations to its right, and the extensive flooding to the west of the village of Argenta to its left. Standing water makes surprise impossible, and, by making fall of shot easy to observe, makes the defender's fire more effective. The gap was roughly two miles wide and eight long. It was flat, low-lying land, crossed by a number of narrow canals and the River Reno, the flood banks of these were major obstacles and could be 30 feet high and 10 wide at the top, and too steep for tanks to drive over. Many had been heavily fortified. The way that the machine gun posts on the flood banks could dominate the flat countryside was to force the attackers to make maximum use of night operations. The Germans had prepared the whole area for defence and had laid extensive minefields.

The Argenta Gap was to be assaulted by two divisions. The main weight of the fighting would be born by the 78th Division. The 56th Division was to make the initial crossing of the Reno and advance along the Lake Comacchio inundations on the 78th Division's right. These two divisions were issued with AFVs of types which were almost novelties to the British army in Italy. The 56th Division received a regiment of Landing Vehicles Tracked Mk4 (LVT4) to carry the troops across the lake and inundations and the 78th Division received a regiment of Kangaroos.

The LVT4s were large amphibious vehicles, 21ft 6ins long and 8ft 2in high. They had been developed by the US for the

174

Pacific campaign where they had proven very useful. They usually carried three machine guns, and were only lightly armoured. In Italy they were referred to as 'Fantails', which is odd because in north-western Europe, where they were widely used at the crossing of the Rhine and other rivers, they were called 'Buffalos'.

As for Operation Cygnet the Kangaroos were to be operated by the 4th Hussars. The regiment's final organisation was:

Two Kangaroo squadrons,	one of 53 Sherman conversions,
	one of 56 Priest conversions,
One tank squadron,	of 17 Sherman tanks.

Only the Sherman Kangaroo squadron was not to be used in this operation, the tank squadron supported the divisional reconnaissance regiment.

A significant point about Kangaroos was the quantity of ammunition and other stores they could carry. In this operation it was planned to carry supplies for 48 hours.

It is of interest to note that in Italy Kangaroos were operated by two cavalry regiments, the 4th and 14th/20[th]Hussars, and each regiment retained a squadron of tanks. This was not the method used in North West Europe, and might have had the effect of fostering tactical innovation.

The problem facing 5th Corps, and 78th Division in particular, was how to keep the offensive moving and not become bogged down, both literally and figuratively. On the basis of its experiences in the previous year in the long advance north of Rome, the division had developed three general principles to be applied to the coming action. These being:

To keep moving at night, because night gave the Germans the chance to re-establish a line or rearguard position.

Forward thrusts were to be aimed at important canal crossings on a line over the minimum number of water obstacles.

German defences in towns and villages were to be bypassed if at all possible.

These principles, while not earth shaking, showed a considerable advance beyond normal infantry procedures.

Eight miles is a long way to have to fight through and because of the difficulties of the task the division took under its command 2nd Armoured Brigade, also 48 RTR, 4th Hussars, and other supporting troops. For the sake of simplicity listing only infantry and armoured units, the division's final organisation was:

Division Commander, Lieutenant General RK Arbuthnott
    56th Reconnaissance Regiment
    4th Hussars, one squadron (Shermans),
    11th Infantry Brigade
        Three infantry battalions
    36th Infantry Brigade
        Three infantry battalions
        48 RTR (Churchills)
    38th (Irish) Infantry Brigade, Brig P Scott
        The Break-out Force
        Two infantry battalions (1 R Ir F, 2 Innisk)
        The Queen's Bays, two squadrons (Shermans),
        51 RTR, one squadron (Crocodiles)
        The Mobile Force, known as 'The Kangaroo Army'
        HQ 2nd Armoured Brigade, Brig J Combe
        One infantry battalion (2 LIR)
        9th Lancers (Shermans)
        4th Hussars, one squadron (Kangaroos)
        51 RTR, one squadron (Crabs)
        One troop of M10 Tank Destroyers
        Reserve Force
        The Queen's Bays, one squadron

176

Two AT batteries
Armoured Troop, RE

The specialised RE vehicles were essential for bridging and bulldozing crossings across the many ditches and canals to be encountered.

The expectation for the 'Kangaroo Army', as it was known throughout 78th Division, was that it would advance on its tracks as far as possible, infantry sections dismounting only if it came under AT gunfire. It could be expected that AT gunfire would be directed at the tanks, as not only were they easier targets, being taller, but would have posed a direct threat to the AT guns.

The Kangaroo Army was assembled on the 10th near Lugo, and the large numbers of AFVs were shuffled into their battle order, a lengthy undertaking. Eight Kangaroos transported an infantry company.

It could be assumed that the Kangaroo Army would be boldly handled. Its commander was the same Combe who had commanded Combe's Force, which had played a decisive part in the Beda Fomm battle. He had been captured with General O'Connor when the Germans drove the British back to Tobruk. Together with O'Connor he escaped, after three years, and was quickly given a command, doubtlessly eager to make his name.

The Argenta Gap battle started on the night of 10th/11th April with an attack by 56th Division aimed at extending its bridgehead across the Reno in a triangular piece of land called 'The Wedge'. Their first move was to secure the area around Menate. To do this one brigade advanced with two battalions mounted on LVT4s across the inundation, another brigade advanced on foot to the west of the inundation. The division was supported on the right by a

Royal Marine Commando advancing on foot along the lake's flood bank.

The operation was a success, despite heavy casualties being suffered by the marines. It seems that the LVT4s were unexpected and the sight of these large machines, trundling out of the early morning mist and gloom, broke the morale of the defenders.

With the first objective secured the two assault brigades moved inland, with one brigade advancing along the road to, and past, Filo. The other returned to the Reno and cleared its northern bank as far as its confluence with the Santerno. It was only after these successful operations that the 8th Army commander, Lieutenant General McCreery, finally sanctioned the Argenta Gap battle.

By the morning of the 12th April the Santerno had been crossed though the right hand Division, 8th Indian, had not been able to construct the planned Bailey bridges. However an Ark was in position by 5:30 am and soon after tanks were crossing to extend the bridgehead. At 2:00 pm orders were received from 5th Corps for 78th Division to pass through the bridgehead and thrust north to Bastia.

At the last moment there was a change of plan. 36th Brigade had been ordered to clear the right bank of the Santerno, so would not need to cross. However, perhaps because the Germans had fought too hard on the Senio to mount much of a defence on the Santerno, it had been found that there was little resistance there so the brigade, with 48 RTR, was ordered to cross the Santerno before 38th Brigade and extend the bridgehead to the west to free up space for that brigade to form up. Due to traffic congestion only the leading battalion of this brigade, 8th A&SH, crossed before 38th Brigade, the delays being mostly due to their accompanying squadron of Churchills. When they did attack, at 5:30, they encountered little opposition and rode into action on the tanks that had been delaying the crossing.

As soon as the Argylls had crossed the Santerno 38th Brigade started to cross. The first infantry battalion, 1 R Ir F, and the Bays crossed successfully but the second battalion, 2nd Iniskillings, was delayed by shelling and general traffic congestion, and it was dark before they crossed so the divisional commander decided that the brigade should laager up for the night.

The Argylls were progressing well and continued as far as San Patrizio where they halted at 11:30 pm. There is no doubt that the Germans were temporarily rattled by the pace of the advance. Some trees had been prepared for felling across the route, but this had not been done. In San Patrizio as the Argylls arrived so did a German 'Rhinoceros' self-propelled 88-mm anti-tank gun, its crew went up to talk to the crew of a Churchill, thinking it was a German tank, and were most indignant to be taken prisoner.

To capitalise on the Argylls' success they were ordered to press on the village of Conselice which they did, and settled down on its outskirts. This village covered some important canal bridges and could be expected to be tenaciously defended. Consequently a second battalion (6RWK) was ordered up. It arrived at San Patrizio at dawn, 5:20, and with its squadron of Churchills proceeded to attack Conselice. At a range of 500 yards the Churchills were engaged by tank destroyers. They knocked out two but the leading troop leader's tank was hit in the turret, killing the officer and the rest of the turret crew. This was seen by some German infantry who boarded the tank and either drove it away or forced the wounded driver to. It was later found abandoned to the north of Conselice. The fight for Conselice then bogged down.

Before dawn on the 13th April, 38th Brigade started its advance. The Break-out Force advanced with two battalions forward, each supported by a squadron of the Bays and a troop of Crocodiles. The plan was to advance between the Santerno and the Fossatone canal for 7,500 yards up to the Scolo di Conselice, a '*scolo*' being a drainage ditch. If a bridge could be secured over this the Kangaroo Army would make a dash for Argenta. The Inniskillings led the attack. For the first 2,000 yards everything went well, then, after they had crossed a small ditch they spotted two German tanks and an AT gun about 700 yards away, by a farmhouse. A troop of Shermans from the Bays was called up, but they were quickly knocked out, so an infantry assault was put in following a short bombardment which finished with smoke. The assault succeeded with a loss of six wounded. The German tanks escaped, the AT gun did not.

The two waterways the attack was to proceed between draw gradually closer together. Initially they were 2,000 yards apart, but about half-way to the Scolo they were only 1000 yards apart so the left battalion, the Royal Irish Fusiliers, crossed over a bridge to the western side. While this was happening the Kangaroo Army was crossing the Santerno.

The next obstacle, the village of San Bernardino, proved difficult. It was attacked from the east by units of 8th Indian Division, and from the west by the Inniskillings, and was cleared by 1:00 pm. Both battalions arrived at La Giovecca before 1:30 pm. Their right flank was covered by some of the division's recce troops, but the left was totally open as 36th Brigade still fighting at Conselice. The battalions were ordered to go firm, even though they had not reached the Scolo, and prepare for the Kangaroo Army to pass through which it did soon afterwards.

This mass of vehicles advanced ponderously. One tank was lost to an anti-tank gun, but resistance was crumbling.

180

There was some determined resistance in La Frascata and one company dismounted to subdue it, which it did and the following company drove through in its Kangaroos. Unfortunately as they reached the Scolo they saw the bridge blown. The company then dismounted and, under covering fire from the tanks, crossed the canal on the rubble of the bridge, and rushed some buildings to establish a bridgehead. A squadron of the 9th Lancers drove along the Scolo to the east and found a partially destroyed bridge. It was still just passable for tanks and by 6:30 pm they had two troops across. These reinforced the bridgehead and the Royal Engineers set to, to build a Bailey bridge.

While the Kangaroo Army had been crossing the Scolo, four miles to its rear the fight for Conselice was continuing. It would require all of 36th Brigade and continue until the next morning.

On the morning of 14th April the situation could be seen to be very favourable for the offensive. Conselice was almost captured and 36th Brigade was exploiting its success and advancing towards the Sillaro. Also the 56th Division had troops north of the Reno advancing on Bastia.

The Kangaroo Army's day started at dawn with infantry patrols feeling their way towards Lavezzola. They were followed by the armour in two columns, one going due north up the main road to Lavezzola, the other looping round to the right to avoid Lavezzola which was known to be heavily mined. Fortunately the Germans had abandoned the area so hastily that they did not have time to remove the *'Achtung Minen'* signs, and there were no casualties caused by mines. The flail tanks cleared large numbers of them.

At 9:40 the Reno was reached. The two bridges, road and railway, had been blown but, at 12:30 two platoons crossed on the rubble to attempt to form a bridgehead. The Germans, true to form, put in a counter-attack and the two platoons were overrun, most of the soldiers taken prisoner. Unfortunately, due to the height of the flood banks, the tanks could not give any fire support. It is only a pity that there was no RE detachment available to correct this.

The position of the Kangaroo Army on the Reno was a salient for only a short time. Contact was soon made with an Italian Combat Group, fighting on the Allies' side, to the right, and 36th Brigade which was coming up on the left. Most importantly 56th Division was approaching from the east and was expected to link up with 38th Brigade around Bastia. However events were reaching a critical stage. The offensive had now reached the narrowest part of the Argenta Gap and the land was most heavily fortified with inundations, earthworks and minefields. Fortunately Italian partisans assisting the division knew routes through the minefields so saving many casualties. It was of great importance to keep the pace up, and waiting for the RE detachment to complete the Bailey bridge might have given the Germans that little extra time to settle unto their prepared defences. Consequently the third brigade of 78th Division, the 11th, was ordered across the Reno where the north bank was held by the 56th Division. It took over the left of that division's front.

The next two days saw a great deal of reorganisation. The most important aspect of this was that the Kangaroo Army was to come directly under the divisional HQ as did the specialised armoured units. The new organisation certainly looked sensible on paper but the London Irish Rifles (LIR) were to switch, as the situation demanded, between 38th Brigade and the Kangaroo Army. This would, on occasions, leave 38th Brigade with only two battalions. On 16th April 56th Division mounted an attack on Argenta, with 11th Brigade on its left. By the evening 11th Brigade with the Bays and the Crocodile and Flail squadrons of 51 RTR, had advanced with two battalions up and one in reserve on both sides of the railway line, and had reached just short of the

Fossa Marina which was immediately in front of Argenta. This canal was believed to be the main German line of resistance. 56th Division had advanced on 11th Brigade's right. During this time the RE had bridged the Reno and the 38th Brigade and the divisional HQ had crossed.

Firm resistance along the canal indicated that a full scale assault would be necessary, and that night a battalion of the 11th Brigade crossed and formed a small bridgehead that held off several counter-attacks. The supporting artillery caused heavy casualties among the attacking Germans. Just before dawn the canal was bridged by an Ark and a troop of the Bays crossed but the Ark became unusable, presumably one of its ramps collapsed. This was repaired later in the morning.

At dawn, 17th April, more infantry crossed the canal, and the full brigade was deployed against Argenta. At around this time troops of the 29th Panzer Grenadier Division were identified among those fighting 78th Division. This was significant as this division was the last major unit of the German reserve in Italy, so it could be seen that the Germans were planning a desperate defence of the Argenta Gap and this emphasised the importance of the bridgehead across the canal.

The first two battalions of the 38th Brigade passed through the bridgehead and advanced roughly north-west gaining 1,000 yards up to the Scolo Arenare. Two of the Bays' Shermans, supporting the Inniskillings, were knocked out by a Tiger during this action. Towards evening the 11th Brigade started to clear Argenta, supported by the Crocodile squadron. This task was complete by 8:30 pm. The town was held against strong counter-attacks early next morning.

The 78th Division now had one brigade, the 11th, requiring relief, one brigade, the 38th, fully committed, and the 36th

Brigade now free, having been relieved on the left by troops from a neighbouring unit. It also had the Kangaroo Army ready to go.

At 2:15 am, 18th April, a gap had been created in the front of the weak 38th Brigade and a battalion of the 36th Brigade, 6RWK, passed through one of the advanced battalions of the 38th Brigade, and advanced in the direction of Boccaleone. As was inevitable with 11th Brigade in action, defending against counter-attacks, troops of 38th Brigade having advanced through 11th Brigade and been heavily engaged, and a 36th Brigade battalion passing through them there was a fair degree of confusion, particularly when German troop movements added to the chaos.

Ninety minutes after 6RWK set off a second battalion of 36th Brigade, 8th A&SH, followed it, veering north to the village of Consaldolo. By dawn assaults on these two villages were developing and suddenly the situation from the German point of view looked very difficult. Whereas in the evening of the 16th the German command's main concern was sending troops down the main road, Route 16, to attack Argenta, now it was necessary to defend that road at two points north of Argenta, where, in the suburb of San Antonio, some German troops were still holding out.

By 9:00am the 6RWK had cleared Boccaleone and captured a self-propelled gun, but Consaldolo was proving a tougher proposition. Due to the inevitable confusion of the night advance the Argylls nearly ran into the RWK, then nearly missed their objective. When they hit it the resistance was fierce, four tanks were quickly knocked out and the fighting in places was hand-to-hand. German artillery fire was heavy and effective. One of the difficulties of confusing night operations like this one is the difficulty the attackers have with providing artillery support.

The deployment the Kangaroo Army followed that of the Argylls. By 10:00 it was out in the open and aiming to cross the Fossa Benvignante a mile north of Consandolo, losing one Kangaroo to AT gunfire en route. By 3:30 pm, having advanced around four miles, it reported the railway bridge as usable but covered by heavy anti-tank fire from self-propelled guns. This held the Kangaroo Army up for two hours.

During this time Consandolo had been captured. It had been a very determined defence and the RAF had been called in and had devastated the village, leaving the bodies of many German soldiers and Italian civilians under the rubble. Despite this the defence held until a planned assault behind a creeping barrage finally finished it. An heroic defence which, like so many other anonymous feats of arms, will never receive the credit it deserves.

At dusk the Kangaroo Army crossed the Fossa Benvignante and the German front started to show signs of disintegration. The tanks and the infantry fanned out to reach Palazzo and Coltra, and three bridges across the Fossa Sabbiosola. The Germans had not expected this turn of speed and two full batteries, one of 150-mm and one 88-mm guns, were captured intact along with several individual guns.

When to move is always a problem for retreating troops, the attackers will usually have command of the air and trying to move guns through choke points, like bridges, in daylight can invite heavy casualties. However holding on too long may result in disaster.

A large number of prisoners was taken. Remarkably reconnaissance parties from some field regiments accepted the surrender of some German artillerymen, saving on counter-battery shoots.

While the Kangaroo Army was having its success north of the Fossa Benvignante, steps were being taken to clear Route 16 so that it would be open for the 6th Armoured Division to use next morning. This task was allocated to 38th Brigade, which had under its command for this operation the RWK from 36th brigade, the Northamptons from 11th Brigade, the 56th Recce Regiment and the 2nd Royal Marine Brigade from the neighbouring formation across the river to the west. They were all directed against the San Antonio suburb of Argenta, and took it after a heavy barrage and vicious fighting. The soldiers, at this time, could hardly be expected to appreciate the German heroics, but posterity should.

The Germans attempted a counter-attack from behind the flood-banks of the Reno close to San Antonio. If successful the manoeuvre would have cut off the Kangaroo Army and re-established the German front, but it failed in the face of the British artillery.

The 36th Brigade, seeing its chance, sent a battalion, the Buffs, north along Route 16 from Consandolo. This battalion started at dusk, and by dawn had covered eight miles and arrived at the village of Benviganate, further on than the Kangaroo Army, and the division could be said to be right through the Argenta Gap. After 60 hours of fighting the division was out in the open, and it had cleared the way for the 6th Armoured Division to launch its pursuit.

After the Argenta Gap the next objective was the Po di Volano, a significant river approximately five miles in front of the Po. It could be expected to be desperately defended to allow the rest of the German troops to pull back north of the Po.

The first contact with the Po di Volano was to be at Cona, nine miles on from Benvignante. During the night of 18th/19th April the infantry of the 38th Brigade kept up the forward pressure. The right battalion, R Ir F, established a firm post to the right of the railway line two miles south of Portomaggiore, the left battalion, LIR now back with the brigade, advanced as far as the twin canals, Bolognese and di Porto, about a mile to the west of the town. Unfortunately both bridges were blown. The 9th Lancers came up at dawn and the tanks and infantry went firm on the south bank.

Between the two infantry battalions 'B' Squadron of the 56th Reconnaissance Regiment, supported by some 4th Hussars Shermans, was trying to cross the two canals in Portomaggiore itself. It was held up by the fire of two self-propelled guns from a strongpoint, Croatia, about a thousand yards north of the town.

The 36th Brigade, including 56th Reconnaissance Regiment, less 'B' squadron, continued north from Consandolo to keep Route 16 clear.

The 2nd Armoured Brigade sent a company of the LIR to assist the reconnaissance squadron in Portomaggiore. They were not successful and returned mid afternoon when, with the support of artillery, smoke and Wasp flamethrowers they established two small bridgeheads over the canals to the west of the town. It was decided to exploit these crossings as soon as possible and 11th Brigade, which had returned to its role as divisional reserve and was close to Argenta, was rushed up to cross the canals, enlarge the bridgeheads and proceed north to cross the San Nicolo canal. To do this it took the LIR and the Bays under command.

Bridging the canals was more difficult than expected and it was not until 9:00 next morning, 20th April, that the advance, two battalions forward each with a squadron of the Bays, could start. When it did opposition was determined and progress slow. By dark the right battalion had almost reached the canal, and the left had linked up with 36th Brigade.

While 11 Brigade was advancing, one company was detached from the Northamptons, who were the brigade reserve, to join the 2nd Armoured Brigade. At midday this company, together with the Sherman squadron of the 4th Hussars was sent to Portomaggiore to assist the reconnaissance squadron in clearing the town and the Croatia strongpoint. This was not achieved and the town stayed in German hands overnight, preventing the construction of a Bailey Bridge for the main Voghenza road.

Things were slow on the right flank, but on the left, essentially Route 16, the 6th Armoured Division was starting to come through. Early morning, 20th April, the first major unit, the 2nd Lothians, arrived at San Nicole Ferarese. With this looming on the left front the divisional commander decided to take advantage of German confusion and try a night assault to gain and cross the San Nicolo canal and exploit to the north.

The assault was to be undertaken by 38th Brigade and two battalions assaulted the canal behind a creeping barrage at 1:30 am 21st April. The troops crossed on the rubble of two bridges. They were supported by two squadrons of the 10th Hussars which had just returned from service with the 56th Division, the Bays now being with 11th Brigade. They crossed the canal mid-morning, as soon as crossings could be bulldozed.

The left battalion, with its squadron of tanks soon captured Montesanto. On the right the land was more open and the tanks were engaged by a self-propelled gun that knocked out two tanks before it was hit in its turn.

This success was mirrored on the right flank where Croatia had finally fallen to the Reconnaissance squadron and its supporting infantry and tanks. Also Runco had been taken, but to get really decisive results the Kangaroo Army had to be launched and as soon as possible.

By midday the bridgehead was large enough to deploy the Kangaroo Army, where it came under heavy mortar fire. The LIR was back with the Kangaroo Army, and unfortunately its Medical Officer was wounded when a shell burst in a tree above his Kangaroo. These vehicles, being open-topped, were vulnerable to air bursts. It is fortunate that shrapnel shells were obsolete by this time. Orders were given for the Kangaroo Army to advance five miles to Cona and Quartesana and seize the river and canal crossings respectively at these places. The Kangaroo Army finally moved off at 3:0 pm in company/squadron groups.

Progress was initially slow, each farm or group of buildings it came across was a potential strongpoint containing guns and panzerfausts, and the infantry had frequently to debus and clear them out. Progress, though, was helped by the RAF flying its 'cab rank' system to provide support on demand. This was essential as the Kangaroo Army had passed beyond the ranges of most of the division's artillery. Even so night was falling and the objectives had not been reached, but the brigade commander decided to press on, attempting a *coup de main.*

Quartesana was rushed by the tanks and kangaroos. It contained three tanks which knocked out two tanks of the 9th Lancers. In the chaos the German tanks and infantry slipped away into the darkness and the bridge was captured intact.

The battle for Cona was more of an infantry fight. The village was covered by a 15-cm gun about 100 yards to the north of the Po di Volano, and the village itself had a sizeable garrison. However the village, bridge and gun were taken by a determined infantry/tank assault. Both bridges had been captured by 1:00am 22nd April.

The two battles had been hectic, fighting at night, the scene illuminated by burning tanks and buildings. The LIR had had an extremely active three days and, at dawn, the battalion was relieved by an 11th Brigade battalion.

While the Kangaroo Army was advancing, and it had covered the five miles in 12 hours, its right flank was covered by the 56th Reconnaissance Regiment, which lifted many mines and overcame several demolitions in order to keep up.

On the left the two leading battalions of the 36th Brigade, with 48 RTR, had made a very impressive march, suffering around 25 casualties *en route*, and arrived at the Po di Volano only a short while after 1:0 pm. The second of these battalions, 6RWK, was clearing the area to the south of the Po di Volano when a Panzer IV trundled into its HQ area. Its commander quickly realised his mistake and the tank disappeared into the darkness before it could be engaged.

By midday on 22nd April, 11th Brigade had passed through the Kangaroo Army's bridgehead, taken 56th Reconnaissance Regiment under command, and advanced north. They came across strong resistance but this was quelled in conjunction with units of 56th Division approaching from the south-east.

The failure of the German defence of the Po di Volano was a disaster for the troops trying to cross the Po, and on the morning of the 23rd their resistance started to crumble. To the 78th Division's left tanks of the 8th Indian Division reached the Po at 10:45 am, further to the west the 6th Armoured Division arrived there at 10:55. However in front of the 78th Division there were still German troops determined to make a fight of it. All three brigades advanced to the Po and all three had serious fighting to do to get there.

Dawn on 23rd April saw the 11th Brigade with a substantial bridgehead over the Po di Volano at Contrapto and Sabbioncello, in conjunction with the 56th Division. While 36th Brigade was advancing north-west in the direction of Ferrara on the flank of 8th Indian division. It was time for the 38th Brigade to move. The critical factor was bridging the Po di Volano. This was done at Giacomo, putting the brigade on the right of the division, but not till 11:0 pm. The two infantry battalions, each with a squadron of the 10th Hussars, were first to capture Saletta, then split, the right battalion to make for Zocca on the Po, and the left battalion, Ruina, just short of the Po, on the Canal Bianco. This advance took longer than expected. Saletta was reached at 2:0 am, but not cleared till 5:0, then the advance continued as planned. The 11th Brigade and Bays made similar progress to the west. The 36th Brigade was taken out of the fighting in order to be ready to cross the Po in Fantails, an operation which was to be cancelled.

Shortly after midday on 24th April the Kangaroo Army moved off. This time, under HQ 2nd Armoured Brigade were three squadrons of the 9th Lancers and the 4th Hussars tank squadron, as well as the LIR. Its route took it through the 38th Brigade's bridgehead then west to sweep the division's front, operating between the Fossa Lavezzola and the Canale Fossetta, the area south of which belonged to the 11th Brigade. It was to sweep towards Ferrara

The brigade covered around five miles against steadily increasing resistance, and, at dusk, around 6:0 pm, the 9th Lancers encountered some tanks and, for the loss of two Shermans, knocked out seven Panzer IV's. The brigade was strung out over 4,000 yards and, against a determined and fully functioning enemy would have been in a vulnerable position, but there was no doubt that the German command had lost control. Immense columns of vehicles and stores were being set on fire by the Germans, and the RAF was doing its bit, apart from that the landscape was covered with burning buildings. This situation was confirmed by Corps HQ at 11:30 pm who passed on an intercepted German message which said, broadly, *'every man for himself'*.

As the situation became known the Kangaroo Army was ordered to swing due north. This was easier to say than do, so many sub-units were involved in small and confusing actions. Consequently a halt was called, the brigade collected, and at 1:30 am, with two companies forward, still mounted, behind a creeping barrage with tanks following, the brigade started north.

Dawn, on 25th April, amid scenes of staggering destruction, saw the end of resistance south of the Po.

As the previous pages have shown the Kangaroo Army was involved in four break-outs, being:

On April 13th/14th, an advance of	8 miles to the Reno,
19th, "	6 miles to the Fossa Benvignante,
22nd, "	6 miles to Cona and Quartesana
24th/25th, "	7 miles to the Po.

The total distance covered in these advances was 27 miles and all these advances, except the last, made against determined resistance by good quality troops in prepared positions.

The distance travelled by the Kangaroo Army was not as significant as was the disintegrating effect its advances had on the German defenders. It did not give them the time to settle into their next line of defence, and prevented the orderly retreat of their units. The Kangaroo Army normally started its advances during daylight even if it did sometimes continue after dark. Conversely the marching infantry preferred to operate at night. These two opposing modes of action resulted in the German defenders getting little rest.

After each of its short advances it had to stop to let its flanking units catch up. Bypassed centres of resistance, like Conselice, could be completely surrounded and snuffed out with far fewer casualties than would have been the case if they had been taken by advancing troops.

Of particular interest was the organisational structure of the Kangaroo Army, in that, as required it was under either the Division or the 38th Brigade, and it either included, or did not, include the LIR. Exhausting no doubt, but it did make the best use of everyone and everything.

Finally it may be said that the German force was in a state of collapse which, while true it was certainly not obvious from the point of view of the 78th Division.

Comments

Probably the most remarkable aspect of the history of Kangaroos is that it took so long for the need for them to be recognised. By the end of the Great War the Tank Mk IX was almost in production. One version of it could carry 30 soldiers and had loopholes so that they could use their rifles from inside it. With the end of that war the concept was dropped although transporting troops in lorries became common. When it became obvious that the cavalry must be mechanised some light personnel carriers were looked at as replacements for horses, but that idea also was dropped. However what were to become known as Bren Gun Carriers were developed, and each infantry battalion had a platoon of thirteen of them. They were found to be very useful, but being open-topped, thinly armoured and under-powered, they were best not used under direct fire.

Consequently the army embarked on the Normandy campaign with no particular desire for APCs, and it was really because of the foresight of some imaginative senior officers that it got those that it did. Perhaps better use of Kangaroos could have been made in North-West Europe, but as this chapter has shown there were too few to have made a significant difference to the campaign.

Better use certainly was made of Kangaroos in Italy where they were combined with tanks and supported by ground attack aircraft, but that was just before the end of the war, so this tactical innovation could not have full advantage taken of it.

Probably the finest concluding remarks about Kangaroos were spoken, on 11th May 1945, by Lieutenant-Colonel Churchill, the commander of the Canadian Armoured Carrier Regiment, on leaving it shortly before it was disbanded:

'...we have also been instrumental in saving the lives of countless soldiers who, without the Kangaroos, would have had to advance on foot unprotected from enemy fire. It is most comforting to reflect that many Canadian and British soldiers are alive today because of this Kangaroo regiment.'

Chapter 10: Conclusion

The previous chapters have shown the evolution of British armour as deployed in the direct support of infantry. Its account has started with the heavy tanks of the Great War. These were large and generally unsatisfactory vehicles that the German AT defence was becoming able to cope with. It has considered the post-war difficulty of supporting infantry with comparatively fast Medium Tanks. It looked at the half-formed inter-war ideas that believed that large numbers of small tanks would be able to overwhelm a defence. The idea was dropped as a result of the Spanish Civil War experience but it had spawned the Matilda I. This led to the other 'Infantry Tanks'.

The Infantry tanks, being almost 'invulnerable on the battlefield', led assaults during the first two years of the Second World War, but all too soon developments in AT defence removed that invulnerability. The result of this was that artillery reasserted its tactical dominance and there would be no assaults until the defence had been prepared by artillery, but even then tanks were halted by mines and a new type of AFV was required to clear a passage through minefields. This was the start of the development of specialised armour. It was soon seen that, if the defence was properly set up with field fortifications and minefields, the attack was led by specialised armour supported by Infantry tanks. Otherwise, if the defence was only hasty, then it could be assaulted by Infantry tanks, these functioning more and more like Cruisers.

The best possible way of helping infantry forward is to carry them in armoured vehicles and, when the objective is a fortified position, the assault of Blerick provides a good model. However it must be emphasised that gaining absolute superiority of fire is essential when deploying Kangaroos in this way.

For mobile warfare the lessons and experience of the war were less conclusive, particularly as in North-western Europe the vast bulk of Kangaroo usage was merely that of armoured lorries, and this was true even when a battalion in Kangaroos was attached to an armoured brigade. The exception was the 4th Armoured Brigade which formed two infantry/armour battle groups, but further tactical evolution along these lines was curtailed by the war ending. That the APC regiments contained only Kangaroos tended to make them function as lorries whereas the organisation adopted in Italy, where the cavalry regiments operating Kangaroos retained a squadron of tanks, may have resulted in more ambitions usage.

This greater ambition, and flexibility, was displayed by the 78th Division which mechanised most of a brigade. Its operations in the Argenta Gap battle saw a series of short break-outs in co-operation with the other brigades of the division. This was a slow method, but it ensured that the enemy was kept off balance.

A British armoured division in mobile operations would advance with a squadron or two of tanks leading, followed by the same carrying infantry, followed by infantry in TCVs (Troop Carrying Vehicles, lorries) unless the infantry was the motor battalion which had, by the end of the war, half-tracks. The advantage of this method was speed, there were fewer vehicles involved. Unfortunately as soon as the division came under fire the infantry dismounted and, because the infantry was usually far from the enemy and, instantly, out of contact with the tanks, the operation bogged down. The 7th Armoured Division improved on this by mounting its infantry in Kangaroos, but only managed to use their Kangaroos in the armoured lorry mode before the end of the war.

It is worth noting that, as the war ground on, the Germans became less interested in making deep 'blitzkrieg-type' thrusts, but preferred to make simultaneously a number of short thrusts, which in at least some cases would make surprise easier and would prevent the defenders moving troops laterally behind the front so making his defeat easier. Perhaps the best use of Kangaroos would, in the early stages of operations, what Field Marshal Montgomery would have called the 'crumbling' stage, have been in the 78th Division mode, but once the enemy started to weaken, in the armoured division mode. This, of course, assumes that there was a choice, and there was a vast number of Kangaroos available.

Unfortunately post-war British practice gives little clue as to thinking about Kangaroos. The vehicles existing at the end of the war were phased out. The armoured divisions were restructured into tank-heavy formations appropriate for counter-attacks and the new APCs were wheeled, useful for colonial wars but not so good for accompanying tanks.

Sketch Maps

Sketch 1
The Battle of Cambrai

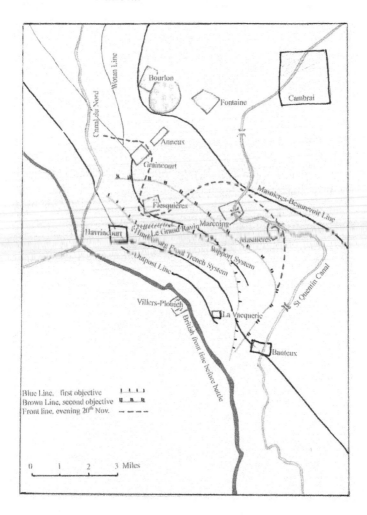

Sketch 2
The 13th/18th Royal Hussars at La Bijude and Epron

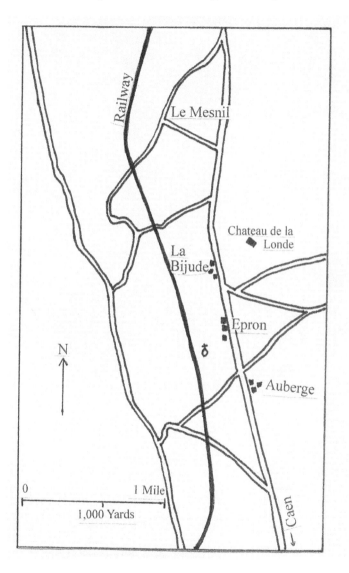

199

Sketch 3
The 6th Guards Tank Brigade at Caumont

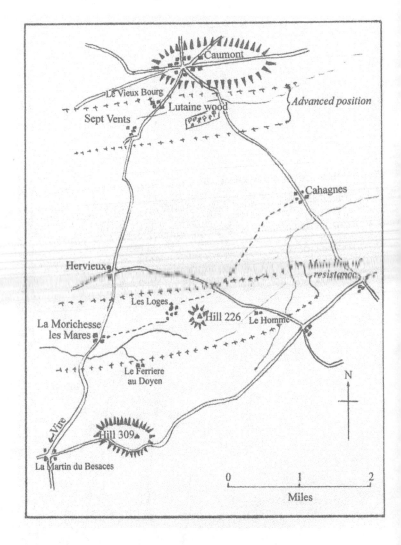

The defences, drawn over a sketch of the modern (2001) road map.

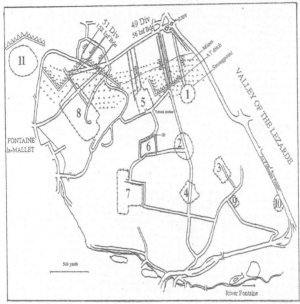

Sketch 5
Operation Guildford

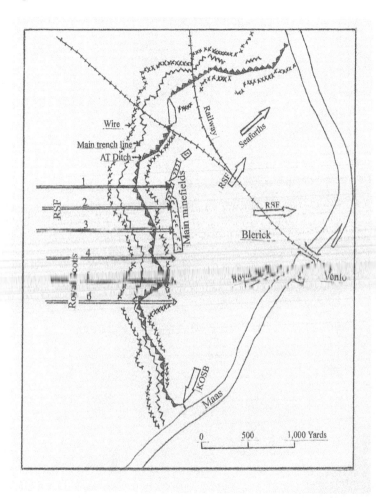

Sketch 6
Operation Buckland

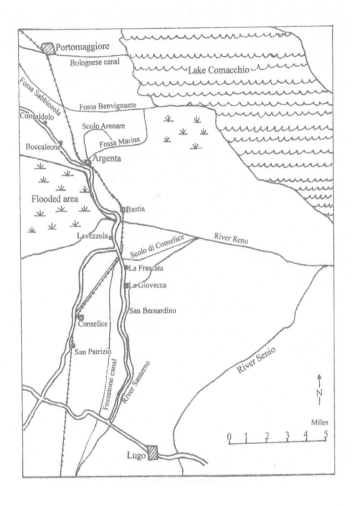

Sketch 7
Operation Buckland

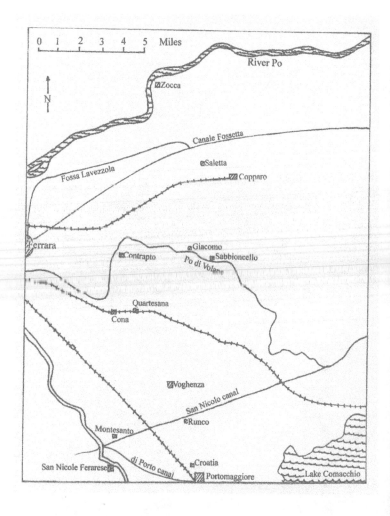

CPSIA information can be obtained
at www.ICGtesting.com
Printed in the USA
BVHW071927180419
545907BV00002B/182/P

'Infantry Tank Warfare' is the term used in this book to describe the use of armoured vehicles to support infantry in the attack. Although there are chapters covering the experience of armour in the Great War, and inter-war developments, the greater part of the book covers the Second World War. Within the main theme there are three topics: infantry tanks, specialised armour and armoured personnel carriers. Each topic is studied separately by considering the vehicles involved, the manuals for their use, and the actions they were involved in. The result is an appreciation of the fine achievements of the British armoured forces.

It is important to note that the book restricts itself to a detailed investigation of the British experience, only occasionally referring to foreign armies and then purely for comparison.

This book, in style and content, has been written as a companion volume to the author's 'Cruiser Tank Warfare'.

ISBN 978-1-78507-158-4

9 781785 071584

90000

www.newgeneration-publishing.com

New Generation Publishing

Infantry Tank Warfare

(Revised and enlarged)

John Plant

387·6